Books by Ray R Wise

* Forthcoming

<u>External Cities Series</u>

Megotholis

*Tricromolis

*Pyfermolis

*The Forbidden City

<u>My Wolf Within Series: From the Journals of Wilhelm Von Krieg</u>

Book One 1750-1783

*Book Two 1784-1820

*Book Three 1840-1882

*Book Four 1902-1946

*Book Five 1947-2012

<u>That One Dark Night Series</u>

The Mountain of Terror

The Forest of Horror

*Return to Terror Mountain

*Haddendrak's Machine

*The Realm of Omnuzuk Ramokor

MY WOLF WITHIN

From the Journals of Wilhelm Von Krieg

Ray R. Wise

Wolf Within: From the Journals of Wilhelm Von Krieg 1750-1783

By Ray R Wise

© August 2016, October 2020 Okt31 Media Publishing

All Rights Reserved. No part of this book may be reproduced in any form by any electronic or mechanical means, including information storage and retrieval systems, without permission in writing from the copyright owner, except by a reviewer who may quote brief passages in a review.

All characters appearing in this work are original. Any resemblance to real or like persons, living or dead is purely coincidental.

All Cover designs and artwork created by Ray R Wise

Second Edition October 2020

ISBN# 9798693076051

Dedicated to my father

Robert Wise

Who introduced me to the wonderful worlds of science fiction, fantasy, and imagination.

ACKNOWLEDGEMENTS

I would like to give thanks to everyone who helped make this book possible. Thanks are due especially to Lois Bartolini and Robert Wise whose input and insight contributed to the story in so many ways.

INTRODUCTION

Wilhelm Von Krieg has been one of the most iconic and controversial figures within the communities of occultism. With writings dating back as early as the 18th century, Von Krieg portrayed himself as an established physician of medicine, while concealing his crimes as a mass murderer. Historian experts, through document analysis, have proven Von Krieg did not only exist but resided during said dates and locations across Prussia. However, evidence disproving or confirming his shapeshifting rituals is yet to be found, thus stirring years of debate and adding speculations to the already contentious issue.

Therefore in publishing Von Krieg's works, we feel it best, to begin with, his assumed final memorandum. Assumed, meaning the following entry, though been found on the last page of journal five, references no actual date to when it was written. Paleography states the entry in question predates Von Krieg's fourth journal thus suggesting he may have written it as a separate entity.

We take full responsibility in informing the reader that all material is unaltered, (though translated loosely) and describes heinous acts of schadenfreude and extreme violence. We have openly published this information in the hopes of education and deny use for any means of profit or entertainment.

Dr.Sarah Carter

International Investigations Community

Last known entry, date not recorded

I am a werewolf, cliché? It might be for an introduction, but there is no better way to introduce myself. Perhaps if I start from the beginning it would bring things into a brighter perspective. My name is Wilhelm Von Krieg and I was born in 1733, Weimar Prussia with a father that was a gentry (Junker). He possessed much land in the east where peasant leaders supervised our fields and tenant farmers handle the crops. I had a good childhood, first-rate education, and some very dear friends. The typical life of the upper class that was until the night I was mauled.

This is where my story takes a drastic turn and why I began to record my chronicles at that time. Everything else just seemed to be so insignificant before the event. Nevertheless, the reason for publishing my journals was to bring an understanding of my condition and awareness of our ancient folklore.

Labels such as Therianthropic, Lycanthrope, and shapeshifter are all classic names created centuries ago by the ignorant or gothic romantics. These deluded interpretations later developed into beliefs, which lead us into dark times, not unlike that of the witchcraft trials. Valais and Vaud (what you now call Switzerland) are where our origins can be traced back too. From the 15th to 18th-century allegations of Lycanthropy were mixed with accusations of wolf riding and even wolf charming. (For example the case of Peter Stumpf, It is a virtuous read and I highly recommend it.)

In later years, myths of our existence developed into a form of entertainment. Radio and film displayed our kind as demons and grotesques beasts. Popular culture spawned titles like "The Wolfman" and "Werewolf" which to this day are still used to describe us.

Of course, many different languages also gave us many names, Hombre Lobo, Loup Garou, and Mannaro, the truth however is that these appellations were created by those who have never actually encountered one of us face-to-face. To each other, we are simply called "Wolf". A term used loosely to explain the actual affliction within ourselves.

You see the "Wolf" is practically one-half of a split persona for those who are infected with the disease. We all contain a beast within ourselves, bitten or not, but the infection allows it to surface.

The fact is we infrequently change at every full moon or new moon; it is far more complicated than that. Though the moon is a great element in this factor, the earth needs to be a certain distance from the sun and the air must be precisely right.

We do possess a rare gift of knowing when a full moon will occur weeks before it is seen. We can also prepare for hunts and plan attacks with the greatest of stealth and speed, hence why the public rarely sees us. No, I take that back, the public has indeed seen us, and on more than one occasion. The average person has probably encountered at least four of us in their lifetime though completely unaware.

We are in reservations, sanctuaries, zoos, and of course in the wild. You might ask how this could be. There lies the greatest unknown fact of the affliction. A Wolf has a limited about of transformations, after that, we become a complete Canis Lupus. Once completely transformed, all human traits are gone. Though I often wondered if our memories stay with us, I have never met one who has become "Wolfened", but I know those who have.

As for our ways of life, we do not worship some God called Gaia. In reality, many of us come from all types of religions.

We do not base our set of laws on tradition, and certainly not some ridiculous role-playing game created in the 1980s. That fact is there are no rules, we hunt, we kill, we protect our packs, and if we endure, we Wolfened. That is all.

During our transformation into the wolf, we are unaware of our human side. Alert but not in control of our rage, we still recognize, friend, foe, or prey and posses the primal instincts to survive. Once the alteration is done, we revert to human likeness and remember the events of the prior night as if it were only a dream. However, in human form, we still carry the disease and the side effects. (Sense of smell, speed, strength, enhanced vision) These can be debated as either an advantage or a hindrance.

We do live an extended life cycle, some even a few hundred years (like myself) others may only have a few decades before their Wolfened takes place. There is not a set number for the transformations for it depends on the individual but all know the moment will eventually happen. Each time the alteration takes place, we lose something, perhaps a piece of what we once were, regardless, it is our final fate and we accepted it openly.

There are of course many other skills one must obtain and I am not only referring to those while in Wolf form. Whereas hiding a deadly secret one needs to be crafty in human form. *For it is the schemes we create to cover up the acts we perform.* This is where things can get most interesting, oh the stories I have heard of those trying to live in secret against the public eye.

Strength is also a good ability to possess and easily found in numbers. Packs are very common and usually hold territories for protection against town militias and hunters. Being alone is as rare as it is harsh. I pity those who have suffered through isolation.

Therefore, with my vague but informative introduction, I hope you now have a better understanding of our ways. If not, do not dread, you will as you read further into my experiences. Since relocating to the United States, I intend to translate my journals from the original German to English in hopes to be published. (They may be considered great fictional works.) In doing so, I shall exclude a few instances in time from here to there. However, I assure you that no vital events have been overlooked. They are merely periods of monotonous moments or my years of being in exile. During those days I mostly reflected on memories or planning my further advancements. So enclosing all I can say is enjoy my writings, learn from them, and be mindful of the moon.

Dr. Wilhelm Von Krieg.

BOOK ONE 1750-1783

December 16th, Wednesday 1750

Today was the first day of Christmas break from College and being a premedical student at Gottingen University it was a break well earned. Devin, my friend from down the dorm hall, had arranged for a night of drinking and horseplay. This type of ritual usually occurs when we celebrate a brief period of freedom from term papers and lectures. Devin can drink, but I fear for Napes. Napes' background consists of a strict and somewhat sheltered upbringing. He has never drunk more than a few sips of ale, let alone numerous shots of whiskey. I predict the night will end in carrying him home down the alleyway. Kirk will be joining us later in the evening, He on the other hand can hold his liquor, but it is his schemes I doubt. Kirk is the one in the group that always seeks for an adventure but succeeds in us getting into some sort of trouble.

For instance, his latest debacle he acquired a saddle that he proclaimed was made from the finest leather in France. He exchanged a hefty amount of silver for it from the local constable. Well, it turned out not only to be inferior but had literally disintegrated on its first ride and was illegally obtained. Leave it to dear Kirk to sell stolen goods to the authorities. We had to hide him for about a month until the incident had blown over. I hope tonight will be less troublesome and more merriment will ensue. I so look forward to Christmas. I do not know what it is, perhaps it's the residents in this town consumed by joy and kindness, or the simple awe of the white snow covering the courtyards. Something about Christmas warms the heart and fills the soul. Though tomorrow I am sure, I will feel quite different. I foresee a possible repercussion from an overindulgence of alcohol, followed by many hours of convalescence.

MY WOLF WITHIN 1750-1783

December 17th, Thursday 1750

Yesterday was a wicked time. My head is still throbbing and my vision seems to be compromised. I don't know if I am still intoxicated or not. As I wrote in my previous entry, a night of drinking did indeed occur, and far beyond my expectations. It is of pure wonderment that we are not in the infirmary after consuming that much alcohol. Devin of course was the worst, how that man could still stand up straight by the end of the night was astonishing. Napes didn't make it past 9 o'clock as predicted and needed to be carried home.

Luckily, his dormitory mate had attended the same festivity and managed to discipline himself as to not consume any liquor. He was a far better man than any of us at the time and volunteered to assist Napes home. I was reassured, but Devin was too intoxicated to notice his absence.

Kirk also managed to leave the party but did return just as we realized he had left. He had brought with him a Fraulein (very beautiful) and claimed she was his new mistress.

Her name escapes me, Greta perhaps. Kirk stated she was a dancer with a Wanderbuhne and could grant us seating to their play this Friday. It was free of charge as long as we would convene in the pathway behind the local school's gymnasium. (It was where they would be performing.) I envisioned us standing in the back alley, during a blizzard to wee hours of the night, never gaining access to anything. I told Kirk I would pass on this adventure, but of course, he persuaded me with his arm over my shoulder and a proclamation of how important our friendship was to him. He was my friend undeniably and soon I would be on my way home for Christmas. Therefore, I figured I would make the best of it before I departed and assured Kirk I would be there. Although I have not seen or heard from him since yesterday, I will still give him the benefit of the doubt and keep my word.

December 19th, Saturday 1750

Well, I was correct; I had suffered the fool again. I had met Napes outside the gymnasium at the precise time as requested, but neither Kirk nor Greta had ever shown. Napes and I stood by the rear entrance for two hours until Kirk finally arrived. He presented the excuse that the woman had been cut from the show at the last minute and retreated in a fit of despair. He had chased after Greta, later caught up to her at her place of residence, and in a fit of passion indulged in a sexual encounter.

His story was too detailed as most lies are and it was that moment that I realized the woman had never been in the play in the first place. It had been a rouse just so Kirk could bed her. Perhaps Napes and I showing support for this woman somehow gave Kirk the upper hand with her. Nevertheless, we were the pawns once again in his twisted world of schemes and I had had enough.

I told him Napes and I stood in the chilling cold for hours waiting for his arrival but he repeated it wasn't entirely his fault, I might have believed him but based on his past with other incidents ending like this one my anger took hold of me. I shouted that I was displeased and that our friendship was not as important to him as it was to Napes and myself. I then proceeded to leave but Kirk tried to stop me and it was then that I smelled alcohol on his breath. He was drunk and this reassured that my intuition was right. He had been drinking with this woman in a warm cottage or perhaps a room in a hotel with no regard for his friends freezing to death. Kirk had been swept up by this Fraulein and had completely forgotten about us. I can understand that since the company of a beautiful woman has overwhelmed me on a few occasions but I never lied about it. That is what made me angry, in a moment of memory relapse, Kirk had recalled Napes standing in the cold and instead of admitting his error, he would try to play us as fools. I was appalled by his ego and pulled my arm away from his grip. He was indeed intoxicated thus slipped on the ice and fell on his back. Knowing he was uninjured, I snickered but as he staggered to one knee with the help of Napes, my anger returned. I walked off and all I heard was a drunken shout of our friendship ending because I was a prude of some sort. As I kept on walking, I headed down another alleyway and back to my dorm. This was when things took am outlandish turn.

I swear I had thought about dismissing the rest of the night as a figment of my imagination. Perhaps the winter snowfall distorted my vision or my anger just had gotten to me. I even pondered not writing about this in my journal and ending the entry as a botched night, but I know I saw something. It was something peculiar, not natural in the distance and up the road. I can only describe it as being large and beast-like as it moved swift through the shadows. I felt that it saw me as it disappeared around the corner.

I wanted to pursue it, make sure I had indeed seen something as the voice in my head warned me to stop. I of course did not listen and followed this bizarre creature down another alleyway. I felt a streak of fear as I heard growls and groans come from around the way, but I could not stop myself. I continued, and that is when the bright moon broke through the clouds and lit up the area. I froze once my eyes fully gazed upon it. Its breath was smoky and danced in the cold air. I saw its snout, a dog, or a wolf-like thing on its hind legs. It was some sort of beast I am sure of it. As horror and wonderment overcome me, I decided to go home immediately.

However, I often thought about it throughout the night. It was frightening and confusing but also intriguing. I must know what the creature is. Tonight I think I shall search for it again.

December 21st, Monday 1750

It seems my life has taken an unfortunate turn as for this morning I awoke in the infirmary. The nurse informed me that I had been unconscious for the past few days and sustained multiply injuries. I have two deep wounds on his chest and my arm had been ravaged thus bandaged up to the elbow. A few scratches on my head are also dressed and I feel extremely fatigued. I was happy that Napes and Kirk had come by earlier to check up on me and Kirk had apologized. He was sincere and wanted to reconcile, we did, and then he asked me if I remembered anything. I told them I did remember finishing my studies and then ate a late dinner, afterward, I prepared for a night out and grabbed my coat. (Here is where I became dishonest. I told them I was going to the library but in reality, I was searching for that creature. I could not tell them the truth; they would think I was mad.) As I headed on my way, the bright moon again lighted up the night, and then it is all a blank. As if, I lost a moment in time.

I woke up here. They said a stranger had found me battered, beaten, and brought me in. I remember the nurse running to get the doctor as I opened my eyes, then Kirk and Napes visiting in the late morning, claiming I was in a coma for two days. Then earlier this afternoon a wet towel had been placed on my forehead due to a fever. They expected me to have frostbite or some case of pneumonia but somehow I was completely healthy, though slightly drained. Napes had been kind enough to fetch me my journal, thus why I can write this down today. My thoughts still seem to be erratic, out of order and the image of that beast still haunts me. The beast, could it be the reason why I am in this condition? Why I am bedridden? Could it have attacked me? If so then I did not imagine anything, and it is indeed real.

The doctor told me that the authorities would be here soon for questioning. What will I tell them? They will commit me to the insane asylum if I tell them what I know...or think I know. I will make a statement that I never witnessed my attacker due to being assaulted from behind. A believable lie, but this will not calm my nerves or help my injuries. Nonetheless, I must hide the truth.

December 22nd, Tuesday 1750

I was right. This morning the local constable visited me and wrote down in his notebook the events I tried to remember. I told him some truth, how Napes and I quarreled with Kirk a few nights ago. That I walked back to my dorm and the next night I planned to study in the library. After that, I could not recall anything. I did fabricate a small anecdote of how I saw a man walking in the distance, but only sending them on a false trail.

He wrote down what I said, but continued to ask questions about the alleged man I claimed to see. He knew I was hiding something, after all, why would a student claim to study on Christmas break, but I had to stick with that excuse to confirm my story. I knew he was sensing a hint of deceit but it was dismissed as he informed me of something very disturbing. It seems my wounds were the work of some sort of animal. My medical report documented me as having claw marks and teeth indentations.

I of course was terrified, as my assumptions became truth. That beast had caused this, but how would I explain it to them or what it was I saw. All I could do was lay there as my mind drew a blank. I simply told him I was not aware of any animal, especially one that large. The constable of course did not believe me, so I told him I began to feel fatigued again. The nurse was kind enough to escort him out but I know he will return with further questions. I hope that I will regain my strength by Christmas Eve and be at my family's home miles away from the University. This thought gives me pleasure. I think I will rest now.

MY WOLF WITHIN 1750-1783

December 24th, Thursday 1750

It is Christmas Eve at last! I have arrived at my home in Weimar just as I had hoped but not without some controversy. First, it seems my wounds had healed quickly, far too quickly. Secondly, I have gained more muscle mass while lying in bed and thirdly I did indeed contract pneumonia but made a full recovery. The rate at which I had healed was debated but eventually dismissed due to my youth. At least that is what the doctors stated, however a few of them insisted I stay longer. Luckily my mother, being the strong woman she is, explained to the hospital that her son was to attend Christmas Eve dinner and if he wasn't present there would be hell to pay. In fear of my mother's wrath, they agreed to release me and here I am.

I must admit, I feel quite rejuvenated, so well rested, and alert. It was as if my head had been underwater, hazy, or my senses had been diminished my entire life. I have awakened from a slumber and now I hear, see, and smell things I never noticed before. I cannot explain why my senses are so heightened, but it is wonderful. I am surprised at what a few days of sleep and good food can do for one's health. I do seem to have become more sensitive to heat, for the fireplace is too intense for my taste. I am forced to sit on the couch, which is farther away from its firebox than my usual chair. Tomorrow is Christmas and my brother Adolf will also be returning home from his university. He should be here early morning, afterward, we'll attend the later Christmas mass then visit our relatives on the other side of town. The entire family will be together. It is good to be home.

December 25th, Friday 1750

It was a wonderful Christmas morning. Mother made a scrumptious breakfast and then we attended mass. The church service was enlightening. Something about Christmas makes you see the good in all men. The snow was so majestic and beautiful, and being in the company of family, I indeed thought this would be the best Christmas thus far, and it was, until later that night. A friend of mothers had invited all of us to a party across the way, so after our family affairs, we attended with good spirits. I had not been to a gathering like this in rather some time so I was looking forward to the celebration. There was a buffet and the servants were very attentive to our needs. I had met Mr. Engel Aeschelman who was an executive that spoke of new inventions and travels to a new world. Something about colonists and war, and if they were to break away from England it would be of great opportunity. I found this new world interesting but for now, Prussia is where I shall stay. Mr. Aeschelman was rather boring and I tried to be polite by looking interested in his rambling of percentages, yearly earning, and returns on investments. I feared my performance of trying to be fascinated failed because I was too busy noticing a very ravishing young woman from across the room. Aeschelman then inquired about my profession and I told him I was a student of medicine.

In truth, my studies seemed to slip second on my list ever since my incident. The beast I saw still haunted my dreams and with these new senses, everything became more captivating, but the party was not the place to discuss such a matter. Aeschelman then informed me his brother Dierk was also a medicine man and had graduated from Gottingen a few years ahead of myself.

Dierk was attending the party as well but at that, moment was not in our company. Aeschelman did however notice that I was taking a liking to the woman across the room and he beckoned her over. He introduced her as Rebecca and of course Dierk's girlfriend. I found this annoying but kept my composure. Rebecca informed me they had been courting for two months and Dierk was present, conversing with the other guest. Just as the devil would have it, at the exact moment he approached us.

As God as my witness, I had never felt such a familiarization towards anyone. It was a very recognizable and yet primal sense, I knew him, but could not recall ever meeting him until now. I felt aggressive and nervous as if my life was being threatened. It was then something took hold of my senses and I tried to contain myself without either ripping this man apart or running towards the door. I noticed sweat had run down my face so I took a deep breath then exhaled slowly trying to keep calm. Even my heart rate had risen and the room began to feel confined.

Dierk extended his hand as he introduced himself and I firmly responded in kind. I could smell him, something was not right, but yet ... no...He too was ...perhaps... attacked by the same animal as I was... I simply cannot explain it in words. I knew he had felt the same towards me because his demeanor instantly changed as he took my hand. His expression became quite serious as he suddenly told Rebecca to retreat to the kitchen then asked Aeschelman to excuse us both. Aeschelman was confused, but no more them I. I agreed to speak with him in private, for perhaps he knew something more of our bizarre encounter. I followed him outside and into the winter air, but I did not seem to mind the weather. The moon was crescent and I felt my senses intensify. I felt more awaken…no more alive than I ever did. Sweat had soaked my collar and started to drip down my forehead, how is it possible to perspire so heavily in such a cold environment? Dierk must have seen something in me because he grabbed my arm and lead me away from the grounds. His grip was unusually strong and his stench increased, primitive, yet very familiar. I think he said, "Quickly, this way" or something and I followed him to the cartridge house.

I felt faint but he helped me get my footing. He pulled a small plant from his pocket and told me to chew on it. Its taste was rancid, he stated it was called Nightshade and not enough to kill me but it seemed to calm me down. I instantly felt better. Then he said, "I see you have it too" I was not too sure what he spoke about, but he claimed he had been attacked in the same manner as I had. He had heard of my incident and planned to seek me out; it was also he who had arranged my mother's friend to invite us to the gathering. Now it all made sense, well at least from my point of view it did. The Nightshade seemed to curve my yearning to kill, and my hunger was kept at bay. I felt horrible, but Dierk said I looked better compared to a few moments ago. Somehow, he knew how to keep… this under control.

I questioned his knowledge about my odd hunger or my strong urges, he stated again that he had been attacked but some 80 years ago. I could not believe his words for this was all too insane. He claimed he smelled me as well and recognized me as one of his kind. I was not sure what that meant. He then proceeded to tell me that had gone through the exact thing I was feeling and once and a man named Braun Muller had helped him just as he was helping me. Braun he proclaimed was his mentor and taught him about the sickness and our kind and that we needed to stay in groups to be safe. I still did not understand, but he did help me so I listened. Dierk could see I did not fully comprehend what he had told me so insisted we meet with Braun tomorrow, and that everything would be made clear. For now, I was to keep chewing the Nightshade and retire early for the night. Dierk stated he would inform the rest of the guests and my family I had returned home. After feeling better, I agreed and fled back to my house. Along the way, Dierk's words echoed in my mind. I can only hope that I will find more answers tomorrow from this Braun.

December 26th, Saturday 1750

I awoke today feeling somewhat again drained but perhaps that is because Dierk had been tapping on my window at a very early hour this morning. He was standing there in the cold and I quickly got dressed and headed out the front door, hoping my family would not awaken. He looked completely refreshed and bright-eyed as if the events of last night did not happen. He also seemed to be in a hurry, which meant Braun, might not be where ever he was for much longer. I must admit, this was starting to feel like one of Kirks games but not knowing Dierk as well as I did my shady friend I would give him a chance.

There was a cartridge waiting down the street for us, and Dierk explained it was parked by the field not to raise any suspicion. When I climbed into the seat, I could feel the warmth and it was reassuring. He shut the door and proceeded to tell me more about this Braun. How they had been friends for many years and on a few occasions, the man had saved his life. The stories were entertaining, to say the least. Wild parties and encounters with exotic women, mostly these escapades took place at night and under the full moon or so, he claimed. I noticed the carriage picked up speed so I tried to push back the curtains to look, but they had been nailed shut. I had no idea where we were going or even in what direction. Dierk noticed I was concerned, and assured me again that everything would be explained.

It seemed like hours had passed then finally we arrived at a very large and desolated house by a lake. I assumed by the position of the sun It had to be almost noon and soon mother would begin to worry. I hoped this would not take much longer. As I exited the coach Dierk grinned and stated, "We are here" no doubt I thought. The house was large with a porch that needed some work and standing on it was a man escorted by Rebecca, it was Braun. He looked rather short and stocky, much unlike I had pictured him in mind. He came to me as he sniffed the winter air. I started to feel like I did when I first met Dierk, and he noticed it as well. Dierk told me that feeling was normal and that I would learn to get used to it. Braun smiled and told me it was "The Sense" and said it is our awareness, alerting us when others of our kind are near. Usually occurs only when we encounter an individual for the first time. He was right because when Dierk came to my window this morning I did not feel like I did last night. I asked for more Nightshade and Dierk snickered. Braun apologized for his lack of clarity and stated the Nightshade is only to fight off the urges of the moon since it was almost noon there was no need for the plant. My "Sense" on the other hand would need to be contained by my willpower alone. I took a breath, calming myself as he invited us into his establishment. Rebecca remained quiet and started to serve us sandwiches. I welcomed the food since I missed breakfast and took a seat on a very ugly yet comfortable couch. The sandwiches were delightful and Braun seemed pleased that I started to relax. Moments later, we finished our meal and our conversation shifted. "So you're a wolf" was the exact words he said to me. I was taken back and I remember Dierk just looking at me like some sort of child memorized by a new toy. I did not understand what he met, but at that moment, Braun seemed to know me better then I knew myself. I was confused about all of this, the attack, my urges to be...violent...the hunger I felt ...the feeling of losing control. Braun tried to reassure me as Dierk did and claimed it would be all clear once explained.

   Here is where the day got even stranger. Braun spoke of folklore and legend of men morphing into wolf-like creatures during a full moon. He spoke of men by name and their stories of mighty hunts passed down the generations. I was amused until he told me I was one of these men. I of course laughed, and they both looked at me in bewilderment. I meant no disrespect but what was I supposed to take from all of this? Surely, it was a jest, a parlor trick, but then what had I come for? If it were all fables and lore, why would I not have left at that moment? It was because Braun was speaking the truth and deep down I knew it, I only had to listen closely. He continued and spoke of the night he was attacked by the same creature or at least it sounded like the same type of creature who attacked me. It left me for dead, I should have been killed, yet somehow I survived only to awake in a hospital bed with heightening senses. He explained the rage, the urge, how it only comes from the moon, and if we do not hunt we will die. All I could do was ask for his help, if I needed to hunt, I had to learn. What was I hunting? Deer? Rabbit? I was unsure. Braun knew I was naive to all of this and offered to teach me the ways. The first lesson was that we needed to stay together, that "Our Kind" needed to be in "Packs". He then told me that a man named Daniel Bauer was part of their pack once. Supposedly, this Mr. Bauer along with Braun and Dierk had been companions for many years and survived the events that had led them to this house. Mr. Bauer then left for personal reasons, of what he did not say but they were short one member and wished for me to fill the void.

I agreed, for an uncanny instinct ignited and a 'Pack" sounded comforting. After all, how was I going to explain these feelings of rage and the taste for blood to Devin, Napes, or even Kirk? They would not understand and take me for being mentally ill, but the two friends whom I have just met seem to understand me all too well. Braun then told Dierk to get me home before my family started to worry. He wanted me to return tomorrow after nightfall for he wished us to celebrate my joining, and insisted he would have some sort of entertainment planned for us. Dierk agreed and I left Braun's company far more informed about my new way of life. I was also eager to partake in this... entertainment.

December 27th, Sunday 1750

It was a few minutes before 9 p.m. and night had taken the day. I had told mother I was meeting some old school friends at the local tavern for the evening. She worried of course but understood, I did regret lying to her, but I needed to meet with Dierk and Braun once again. I required more knowledge on how to control these urges and educate myself on The Sense. Dierk had once again met me down the street with the cartridge and we had arrived at Braun's a few moments after. This time we had ridden around the back of the house and down a small path towards the lake. I could feel The Sense grow stronger and I became so focused and alert. The smells, all the scents of the trees, the air, and the carriage horse smelled so...appetizing. My god, my thoughts had been devilish and I tried to dismiss them from my head before we arrived by the lake. Braun was awaiting our arrival and greeted us with open arms. He embraced me and called me brother as I noticed the moon. It was the full moon, and its energy seemed to soar through me. Enrich my body and bring a sense of ... invincibility. The sky was black, pitch black with only tiny punctures of light from the distant stars. There was no visible light but my eyes somehow could see all the objects all around me. Braun looked up at the moon with me, and stated how beautiful she was, she? How odd, he worshiped it like some sort of goddess and told me she was the reason for our gift. The giver of our awareness and creator of The Sense, I found that very unusual, but how else would one explain the power we felt. It was acceptable for most religions to worship the moon but I highly doubt they felt as we did. Their fellowship was still based on faith but in the here and now I had could feel far more than that. It was real and with every gaze towards the pale moon, I felt... full of life.

Braun watched me and could sense I was being enthused. He smiled and stated it would be the Awakening soon. What he met... again confused me, but Dierk understood. When I asked about this Awakening, Braun just nodded and said by the end of the night I would know, "Now swim brother". "Swim?" I questioned. It was winter. Braun laughed and assured me it would be all right. I trusted him and removed my dressings then dove into the lake. The water was extremely cold but I seemed to get used it rather quickly. I was a little uncomfortable, but swimming had always been second nature to me. I did not quite comprehend why three grown men were in the ice-cold water, but Braun said, "Think of this as training". I was not grasping any of this until I realized I was warm. My skin had become rough and seemed to hold in the heat. Braun swan near me and instructed I needed to be ready for what was to come. *"The cold water makes the skin tough, and the heart strong, the moonlight in the water is what does this. We call it preparing for the hunt, it's a cleansing, stripping away the smells and confinement of our daily lives."*

Dierk then pointed to the shore where Rebecca was standing on the beach. She was dressed in undergarments and looked liked she had just gotten out bed. Braun gestured for us to return to the shore and I did. I wanted to get dressed, but Dierk told me I would not need them, not need my clothes? This was uncomfortable then Braun told me to get dressed and again in due time I would understand. This whole meeting I started to second-guess, too many puzzles and strange behavior, Moon worshiping, and late-night swimming. How odd but I could not deny the strength I felt.

Rebecca looked a little frightened but Braun told her not to be scared, it would be over very soon. Then he turned to me with a concerned expression, as if giving me a warning. He said what I was about to hear is no reason for alarm, I would understand shortly. He kept repeating this, I would understand shortly, all would be revealed, it was annoying. I then saw him give her a nod and she darted into the woods. Dierk and he waited for what seemed like a few moments then he told me he would bring back food, and that I was to prepare a fire. Wood had been cut and the preparations were already laid out within a small pit near the lake. Again, he warned me of the sounds I would hear and pay them no mind. I was, of course, wanting to go with them but

12

being a guest I knew my place so I began building the fire as requested. He nodded to Dierk and they both leaped into the woods.

Moments passed as I arranged the wood and noticed some oil in a small glass jar nearby. I opened it, the stench was overwhelming, but my reaction to the unpleasant odor was dismissed as I heard the sounds, horrifying growls, and snarls. I ignored them as instructed and poured the oil over the woodpile, which is when something most unsettling came from the woods. It was a chilling scream, a female, Rebecca had screamed, then a sudden silence. It terrified me so much I dropped the oil and the jar shattered, I froze trying to listen again, but it was quiet for a second then howling, a loud howl pierced the night, something beastly but it seemed so natural to me and familiar. I tried to keep my composure and lit the fire with the torch that had been left for me. I sat on a fallen log, my hands shaking, and awaited their return.

It seemed like I waited for hours and I began to think about Rebecca. I grew worried that something might have happened to her or Braun and Dierk. At that moment I decided to inform the local constable, but then from the woods, two beings emerged. Dierk was breathing hard and carried a look of extreme satisfaction. Braun came from my right, holding something that resembled a large slab of meat. When he approached the fire, his appearance shocked me. His chin, hands, and chest were covered in blood. Dierk came into the light and he too was covered in deep red. I stood there petrified, but he guaranteed they were not injured nor was it their blood. That did not comfort me and once again, Braun told me everything would be explained. I became angry and demanded they tell me what had happened.

Braun just remained calm and gave the large slab of meat to Dierk, he put in on the fire, and the smell was delectable. My mouth started to water and the urges grew even stronger. It was drawing me to that slab of meat. I begged for a piece and Braun jested about eating it raw but I did not care. The fire seemed to roast it well and even though I had eaten earlier, I felt this meal would truly satisfy my hunger. Dierk then dived into the lake again to wash off as Braun sat across from me and watch as I devoured my food. He observed with contentment and stated he had me prepare the fire to cook with because I was not ready to eat such things raw yet. He joked about how Mr. Bauer's first encounter with raw meat did not quite agree with him. I joked that Mr. Bauer must be a vegan but Braun smiled and stated that in his defense he never tasted this type of game before and that there was a likely chance I did not either. It did taste different, more tender, and salty than any rabbit or deer but it was delicious. I asked him if it was boar and he snickered, stating it was a delicacy among our kind. It was the essence of our survival. I did not care where it came from and gulped it down.

Though I pondered why they had not hunted with weapons or how they had caught their prey barehanded. I asked Braun and he said that "She was an easy catch being on foot" She? Then I realized...Rebecca...they had killed that woman and I was feasting on her remains. At first, I felt sick, but nausea faded rather fast and I arose, but Braun just told me it was all right and that she had sacrificed herself for us. I was horrified. I had become a cannibal or maybe even a murderer. Dierk then came out for the water and said this was the only way I would understand, it was like I was a pup learning to eat solid foods for the first time, so was the next lesson to learn how to hunt?

I couldn't kill, I wouldn't and I told them that but Braun retorted, stating that if I didn't learn, I would die, for the daily food I normally consumed would now no longer bring me nourishment. I needed something richer, something human. I did feel satisfied and my hunger along with the urge to hunt were restrained, but for how long? My God, he was right! I was in dismay and he instructed Dierk to take me home once again. The long ride was silent, we barely spoke and as soon as I came upon my house, I ran to my room and began writing this encounter down. Her image, her scent, oh that poor girl, poor Rebecca. I will find no sleep tonight.

December 29th, Tuesday 1750

The events that transpired last night were in my dreams, no more like nightmares. That poor girl, they murdered that poor girl. I am unsure as to what to do at this point. Should I alert the authorities? On the other hand, perhaps it is only a joke. Yes, a jest, I didn't, see her death, I didn't witness anything, I never saw a body, just blood smeared on two men, that's it, the meat, it was bear killed hours before. It is a hoax on my part. It has to be.

December 29th, Tuesday 1750 - Second entry

Tonight I knew Dierk would come to my home again so I waited and addressed him harshly. I told him I was aware of their revolting joke and I would not be their entertainment again. Dierk gave me a grin and told me to accompany him to Braun's estate. He said Braun had more to show me and guaranteed that no more jokes were to be played on me. I agreed and took the carriage once again. This time we met at the front of his home, he was sitting on the porch and taking in the night air. It was brisk with a hint of dryness and the moon was full again. A few clouds lingered about its circular shape and as I stared up, I could feel the urge again. It was strong, just like last night, but something was changing. It was almost as if I were excited...or...perhaps motivated to run. I had the vigor and the scents around me were even more incredible. I smelled the flowers, the dirt, the dust on the porch, and the horses in the stables. Bouquets hang back from people long gone and meals served days ago. I could smell Braun and Dierk, they each had their scent, and as a reaction, I sniff the air.

Without even thinking about it, I sniffed the air like a beast, or a dog and Braun laughed. "Good!" he shouted. "You're learning, inhale and focus on what you smell, close your eyes and envision the scent, where it is, what it is, prey or predator, a friend or foe, This will keep you alive." I hoped this was not another trick, but the evidence in front of me proved otherwise. I smelled everything and the sensations were intense and so pleasing.

My concentration was broken as I noticed Braun taking off his coat, then his boots. I asked if we are going swimming once more. Dierk just shook his head, and Braun pointed to the moon and that is when I noticed the clouds had parted. It was full now and I felt something odd, more intense, I fell to my knees as if something had been ripped out from my stomach. Dierk came to my aid but Braun stopped him. "He needs to learn, The Awakening is part of his rebirth". What was he saying? He told me to take off my coat and boots because I wouldn't need them, whatever that meant I didn't understand and I didn't care all I knew was pain, great pain and I screamed, but my voice wasn't my own, it was lower and louder. I felt the power surged through me as Braun slowly approached.

He whispered, "The Awakening is upon you, for the events of last night had to happen in order from you to become whole." I heard his words as my vision burred. He told me that since I tasted the flesh of a human it could now take place. What was this madness? I felt as if this was another trick but all doubt has disappeared as I saw my hand change, it changed. It grew bigger, my fingernails started to stretch and grow like claws, I wonder if I was hallucinating. Was I poisoned? I did not have anything to eat or drink, I felt my mind change as well, more primitive, more instinctual. My worries of school, my mother, the woman, they didn't matter anymore, only...only the hunt...food, but more of the yearning to kill, chase, devour, it was all so overpowering, and then I lost time.

I do not recall much after that, only images in my mind, images of another woman, and streets, more screams, or howling. However what is truly the most terrifying, and I say this to whoever reads these words, is that I awoke with blood on my chest, hands, and face. My dressings were only that of my pants, my feet were bare and my shirt and coat were missing. Braun's house was nowhere to be seen but somehow I was still on the property. I knew this because I could still smell him and Dierk nearby, it was their...territory.

I had to return home, I had to get to my mother's estate before anyone saw me. I ran as fast as I could, not stopping, not looking back, praying for the comfort of my own bed.

December 31st, Thursday 1750 - New Years Eve

I had made it home safe and sound following the events from last Tuesday. I still am shaken and even more so since the local print paper reported that a local woman had been murdered. She was described as being torn apart from an animal of some kind and was found only a few miles from here. The entire town is in an uproar and people are scared to walk the streets. I have not seen Braun or Dierk in almost two days and nor do I wish to. Those two are in league with the devil and their hold on me must stop now.

I also fear for my sanity. I never knew the woman, who was killed, but somehow I possess images, dare I say memories of her face. I can see her in my mind, running, I recall her scent, her fear, and I could smell her blood, skin, sweat, everything, it was so desirable. Her screams call out in mind, screams of panic that only heightened the experience, the experience of the hunt. The blood rushing threw my veins, and the power I felt was incredible true physical power. I had immense strength, speed, and awareness. I moved like water and I swear my feet were in motion with my hands. I remember claws and even fur. Had she been wearing fur? The blood and... her taste, that taste I could still feel on my tongue, it was so gratifying. My God, had I turned into some sort of demon? Has Lucifer himself possessed me? God forgive my actions for I DO KNOW what I have done.

January 1st, Friday 1751- New Years Day

Last night was even more horrendous and repulsive. I thought Dierk and Braun were gone, but they had attended my mother's New Years' Eve gathering. I wished them to go, but Mother, being the sweet and innocent woman she is, ordered me to bring them in from the cold. We had had drinks, but of course, they did not eat. Braun teased that alcohol was good for cleansing the palate just before a good meal. He was making crude jokes and I so wanted him to depart but if I made a scene, it might only arouse suspicion.

Our local constable had also attended the party while a few more men had been on watch. They were in search of the murder and were rummaging around the avenues. It was quite stressful but Dierk and Braun seemed to be unmoved by the whole incident. They carried on as if nothing had happened. My God, there were two murders in my house, and perhaps I might be a third. I drink my Schlitzer beverage rather quickly to calm my nerves, as Mother addressed the New Years Count Down for the party. Everyone raised his or her drinks and laughter spread through the dining room as the clock struck midnight. Afterward, the quartet my mother had hired for the evening began to plays Bach's number five, fitting since had just passed away last July.

I drew in a nervous breath and headed towards the kitchen to be alone for I didn't feel like celebrating. I glanced outside, there was no moon thank god, and I felt no urges or excitement, as I did before. My senses however did seemed to be besieged with cigar smoke and rich alcohol. I headed towards the front room and out onto the porch for some air. There I caught a glimpse of Braun dancing with my mother; I was sickened that such a beast was laying his paws on her. I quickly walked over to him and ask for a word, but Mother accused me of being rude and insisted on finishing their waltz. I could not bear the sight of him anymore and begged her to excuse us. She did but with a rather loud verbal protest and I hoped I did not alert the rest of the guests.

I escorted Braun outside and in a few seconds, Dierk had somehow followed us out. I asked them why they were here. Braun told me that we are now brothers, we are a...pack, and we share things, house, property, even family members. That is where I drew the line and told him that I wanted no part in his bizarre brethren or a cult. I was hesitant to call our relationship anything more than an encounter and asked them to both leave and never return. Their response was...unpleasant as Braun grabbed my forearm. His strength was unbelievable, like a steel trap on my arm and he led me out of the house and into the frontcourt yard.

His gaze was that of anger and questioned. "How is it possible that you still don't understand? You are one of us now and there is no leaving this pack." Pack? He was right; I still did not grasp the meaning of that word. He spoke about how I had my first Changing and ate the flesh of humans. I tasted the blood and experienced the hunt. I was... a wolf...and that is when I realized he was mad.

"You had been blessed with this gift and should embrace it". He mentioned. Dierk mumbled something about me behaving just like someone named Heather. Heather? Who was this Heather? Was that a remark that I resembled a scared female? Braun said that a girl named Heather once ran with them and left the pack as well, she did not survive on her own. I told them I was not a frail female and that I would be quite fine without their influences. I did not believe in this lore of the werewolves. Braun just laughed and stated my beliefs were inconsequential at this point. He asked what I would do when the urge started again and how I would handle my "Wolfened" when it was time. Wolfened? I didn't understand that either and Braun once again reminded me there is so much I still didn't know and needed to be shown. Just then, a constable came walking around the corner of the street and saw us debating. Our voices must have carried and he asked me if everything was all right. I assured him that it was but he showed a hint of doubt as he walked on by. I told them both to leave again because we were attracting too much attention.

Braun then showed me a side of him that I had not seen before and it terrified me. He stated that he did not need to be in wolf form to possess such strength and speed. If I were to alert the authorities again, he and Dierk would ravage the house and take part in consuming everyone's flesh starting with my mother. I was angered by his threat and my emotions overcame my sense of gentleman conduct. I swung at his face with my fist but he was so quick he reacted with a parry and a kick to my stomach. I fell over in pain and Dierk stated that I was too weak for the pack. Braun seemed to agree but was willing to give me one last chance. I did not want this, any of their cults like activity, the wolf thing, the hunts, but it seemed I had no choice. The safety of my mother was now at stake. Braun then declared that they would depart but only if I accompanied them on another hunt in one week at his estate. I was to find my own transportation this time and come alone.

If I were not present, he would slaughter my mother then me. I was horror-stricken but I just wanted them to leave. I got to my feet and agreed in haste, begging them to leave her alone. Braun smiled and patronized me by stating we were still brothers and our promise to each other would be honored until someone betrayed the pack. As I saw them leave, I regained my poise and went back inside. Oh, how I wished Napes and Kirk were here, but both had left to be with their families on the holidays. I so required their company at this moment.

January 8th, Friday 1751

It has been one full week since our last encounter and I hope this is to be just that, our last one. It was about 10 p.m. and once again, I had snuck out of my window and arranged a horse from the neighboring stables. I knew eventually local gossip would get around as to why I required a horse at that hour, but I shall worry about that later.

My mother being in danger was far more in important than a dubious midnight ride. I rode the stallion to Braun's estate and met them both by the lake as we agreed. Braun was pleased to see me, and I told him that I wished this to be our last meeting. He shrugged and stated that after tonight's lesson I would surely change my mind. I snapped that murder was pretty much a breach of contract but he tried to justify the past actions as a need for survival. He avowed murder was a horrible dishonorable act of humans. It was done out of greed, jealously, or just plain insanity, but for us, it was our way to feed and to hunt. For thousands of years, the wolf survived that way, and to do so was to honor the tradition and our way of life. "We take no pleasure in killing, but to survive there was no other way. We only prey on the weak or sick, never children or the strong. It was better for human society this way." The strong may flourish as we kill off the diseased and dying but it was still murder to me. "I am educated in the advancement of medicine and eventually we will cure Cholera, Typhoid, Tuberculosis, and even Smallpox's, then what will we do?" I shouted but Dierk laughed, saying disease will always be around and we were the true cure.

Sick and twisted I thought he was but I silenced my argument, their insanity ran too deep for me to persuade them otherwise. I just wanted to get back home and be rid of these two forever. Braun stood by the fire then began to tell me the history of our kind. He claimed that he was unsure when the first wolf was born, but our origin could be traced back to ancient Egypt. To be honest, his ramblings were odd but interesting, if he had made all of this up, his imagination was impressive, pity he was insane. He proceeded to speak of the moon again and its power. How it enlightens us, heightens our senses, and aids us in the hunt. The he spoke how important a pack was, and that there were also others like us though wished to rule over mankind. (These types were neither as friendly nor forgiving as he was and Braun seemed uncomfortable discussing them.) He mentioned a few humans as well, "Hunters" who were aware of our existence and planned to erase from history.

Braun then paused and sat with a concerned look for a few minutes, before speaking to me again. He spoke of the Changing, and that it was the most important thing a wolf needed to understand so I best pay attention. "One's first time may feel as if something else takes over leaving the individual with only memories of dreams and imagines. The more it occurs the more the body adapts, it becomes less taxing, less painful. We also become more aware of the situation, more attuned to events, and begin to remember every detail of the hunt.

That was exactly what I had experienced, dreams, vague imagines, lost time. I was starting to become unsure of myself. Then he referred to that word again, "Wolfened." I asked him what that meant. He grinned and told me that with each Changing and hunt we become more of our true selves. More of what we all yearned to be until transforming into our final state. It was when one would become wolf completely, returning to human form. I laughed and told him he sounded ridiculous but Dierk stood up, insulted, he swore it was true, and spoke of a man named D'assise who was Braun's mentor long before they had met. This D'assise was a supposed marvel among them but was no longer in their company for he had reached Wolfened. Now he supposedly roamed the wilderness as a full-blooded wolf.

Once again, I found their stories interesting but bizarre and if they assume these tales would keep me from leaving this...pack they would be mistaken. I shifted the conversation and asked why I was here. Braun said it was because he had one last thing to show me. I had hoped to God that it was not another girl; I was relieved to see it was instead his carriage. It was there by the lake but this time without a driver. I stared at it while he spoke of squatters, gypsy's that had taken refuge on his property a few days ago, probably to seek shelter from the winter's cold. Their camp was to the east he declared and his tone was that of disgust. He motioned for me to board the carriage and I did as Dierk followed me inside and Braun took control. As we rode for the short time, I could not help to think we were entering into a confrontation. I noticed once again the moon was crescent and the clouds filled the night sky, it was cold, but dark and I was relieved that the Changing could not happen tonight.

As we came to a stop, I heard whispers and then the door opened. Dierk murmured to be quiet and as I exited the carriage, I could see in the distance a glow lighting up the night sky. It was fire; we had reached the gypsy encampment. Braun climbed down from the driver's bench without a sound and motioned with his hand for Dierk to circle the site. He then gave me a look to follow and I stuck by his side as we crouched down behind and fallen oak. Our position gave me a perfect view of the unlawful residents. There were many of them, men, women, and few children huddled around a large fire, and a few makeshift tents. They were speaking in a strange dialect, perhaps Hungarian. Braun seemed to understand them and eyed a girl. I drew my sight to her; she was young, perhaps the age of 18 or 19 with black hair and sitting by the fire. Her face, a milky white with wide eyes and full lips, she was beautiful. Her scent was even more intoxicating, wild, young... innocent... delicious. I tried to dismiss my thoughts but the smell was irresistible. Braun noticed my satisfaction and stated, "Good, take it in" and I did. I shifted my attention back to the entire group. With every inhale, I could sense their presence, emotions. An old man to the right, his scent was of despair and worry, and an older woman behind him, anger and distaste for their food. There were more of them in tents and with each aroma, I could tell, their age, feelings and I swear their thoughts. How was this possible through smells?

Braun pointed to another female, she too was young, but older than the first and also beautiful. Her stench was of innocent but something was not right, a foul order, something rancid. Braun nodded and told me she was ill. He had smelled it too, disease. Then I realized what was happening, we were on another hunt. I shook my head and told him I would take no part of the killing, but Braun frowned and reminded me of our agreement. I hated him for threatening my family but more so for killing innocent lives. This madness had to be stopped but for now, there was not anything I could do. However, I remembered the overcast and the clouds in the sky. I snickered and questioned how are we suppose to change if there was no full moon to give us power.

I figured I had him outmaneuvered, but he just smiled at my ignorance. His wicked grin was of arrogance and lectured me quickly on the many different types of expeditions that had taken place. There were Night hunts and Pack hunts and what we were taking part in was a Territory hunt. All were executed in the darkness of night and though a full moon did allow us to reach our full potential, it was not needed for one to change.

He then looked outward and with a quick nod, I saw Dierk from across the camp transform before my eyes. Not a man, but standing there was a wolf...no...A wolf thing. It was true...the legends, the folklore... all true. Terrified I watched as Dierk attacked the camp, ravaging the gypsies, their screams filled my ears and I covered them with my hands but Braun pulled me up and forced me to watch. I witnessed the massacre as he scolded me not to fear but embrace it, the screaming, the blood, and then the scent of fear filled my nostrils. I felt something, the pain again, only it was not as intense and tolerable this time. Perhaps it was because of the lack of a full moon. I looked at my hands and saw I too began to transform. It was the Changing happening again, and I heard in a faint voice Braun taunts and then his laughter, then... The imagines that followed I dare not describe in detail, but they are true horrors from hell. I remember chasing the woman away from the camp but not killing her...or I think I did not. I remember her pleads and then a gunshot from a musket. I fled home I think, but this morning I awoke in the stables, my clothes once again ripped, torn, and stained with blood, not of my own.

The sun was starting to rise and Mother had not awoken yet. I treaded lightly into the house and so far without question. That was about nine hours ago. Dear Lord, I have been awake for almost 15 hours now without any sign of fatigue, perhaps I am still in shock. I just hope Mother does not mistake my odd sleeping patterns as sickness. The less she knows the better.

January 10th, Sunday 1751

I had finally fallen asleep yesterday but only to be awoken by visitors. Mother informed me that my friends have come by again. It was Braun and Dierk of course and I met them outside. Dierk looked extremely ill and with anger in his eyes. He was holding his side and leaning on Braun for support. We assisted him in one of the chairs on the porch and I noticed blood dripping down his leg. I insisted he required care and proceeded to fetch my medical bag, but Braun stopped me. His rebuke was harsh, stating he would be all right and the true nature of their visit was because of my actions last night. My performance seemed to be inexcusable and highly frowned upon by my so-called pack. I was ordered to recall the previous night. I did as Braun instructed but only remembered vivid images. He refreshed my memory by telling me I had the sickly woman down and was about to devour her, but then I fled as if I changed my mind.

Dierk called it cowardice and spit at me, suggesting I was the cause of his injuries. I dismissed his outburst and took no blame, however as Braun agreed that I was indeed at fault he began explaining the series of events that took place. I had ceased the chase and the woman had gotten away from me, this caused Dierk to pursue, and that is when her father had shot him. (Thus, the gunshot I had heard.) The ball was still lodged in his shoulder. He looked amiss, but for someone with that type of wound, he fared well and luckily for my sake. I inquired if the woman was all right, it was the wrong question, for at that moment Braun completely lost his temper. Shouting, he accused me of insanity, said I was speaking like a confused hunter that was more concerned about the fox than his hounds. Dierk again spat me and declared I was too weak to join their pack. Braun nodded.

He told me that I was a lost cause and no longer welcome at his estate. Dierk still held his side as he scoffed and proclaimed I would be dead within the year anyway. Braun agreed, lowering his voice but kept his anger. I sensed a hint of disappointment, but I cared not what he thought of me and was relieved to be dismissed. Finally, these two murders would leave me and I could return to school soon. This still did not solve the issue of the girl who had escaped and now people were alerted of our presence. Braun knew it was time to move on and officially banished me from the pack. He told me there shall be peace between us as long as I never spoke of them to anyone.

I agreed for the fear of my mother's safety and apologized, it felt like the right thing to do.Braun then helped Dierk off my porch and without any further word, they boarded the black carriage. I watch them ride away out of sight then slumped back into the chair. I inhaled the cold air deeply in my liberation. It was over and they were gone, hopefully, forever, but their departure did not grant me complete satisfaction, because now, I was on my own.

January 12th, Tuesday 1751

A few days have passed and I have been keeping an eye on the local papers and/or any gossip. Nothing has emerged yet and the press has stated they had not found any clues of the missing woman's case. I still felt sick for her, but I must say I was pleased they had no witnesses. Maybe now I could put this all behind me. The right thing to do of course was to confess, but that would devastate my mother and why should I take the blame for two deranged psychopaths. God will punish them; they will eventually be tried for their crimes. I did learn something most intriguing, Dierk being shot showed me that we as wolfs are not invincible no matter how much strength and speed we possess. We can be injured and perhaps even killed. Interestingly enough, I shall return to the university within four days and there I will conduct tests on my blood. If I am alone I need to learn as much possible, especially if we have any weaknesses.

May 9th, Sunday 1751

I have not written in my journal for some time because I have purposely left it behind at home in Weimar. I have found nothing worth mentioning through my testing, and now I am trying to put this all behind me. I have attended school and focused on my studies, though the events last night may have diverted my intentions. The moon was full again and the Urge came on strong. I tried to resist and stayed in my room but the air carried a scent so pleasing I had to follow. As I did the Changing occurred and then I woke this morning in the field. I was so far away from the university; I must of cover nearly nineteen miles in the night, but the wasn't all. I remember slaughtering a few farm animals... an ox, and... a farmer. That poor man, I can still see the terror in his eyes. I swear I felt as if someone had taken over and the impulse to hunt was so strong, the flesh I craved, the smell of fear overtook me and I succumbed to murder. I committed unlawful death, I took a life..., and it was so satisfying. Now, this very morning, all I can do is weep and try to contain my overwhelming feelings of guilt and shame, perhaps confessing to the authorities would release me, but what would I say? The farmer had been ripped to pieces... how could a man be able to that to another man? They would commit me to an asylum. If what I suffer from is truly, a disease I must find a cure. I must stop myself from killing again. Yesterday I returned home for the spring's break, thus why I am writing this entry now, however when I return to school I shall dedicate my life to finding a solution...an end to this evil...I will find a cure.

May 27th, Thursday 1751

Two weeks ago, I have returned to the university and I have found a reclusive place to restrain myself from further Changing's. I have volunteered to be an Aid at the main library on campus during the late hours. This had granted me access to the basement where I am able to chain myself to a pair of large stone pillars during the nights of a full moon. I have devised a ritual of placing the key to my shackles in a cupboard only a few feet away. As the Changing comes forth, the wolf is awakened and I am overtaken by rage, hunger, and instinct. It does not realize that its freedom is within a few steps away. In the early mornings, I unchain myself and escape unnoticed. Though successful, this seems to be my only progress in restraining my condition. My research in the way of medicine has been inconclusive. This disease seems to elude me even with the most advanced equipment at my fingertips. I had reached only dead ends but I shall not renounce my efforts. Perhaps I am just looking in the wrong direction. I will ponder this more tomorrow after my finals.

June 20th, Sunday 1751

I have decided to stay on campus for the summer and continue my studies, but regret that I have not progressed any further in my research. I have tested my blood, done experiments on my skin, teeth, and hair but found nothing. I cannot explain it; perhaps this is also due to my lack of energy. I have been extremely fatigued in the past weeks. The food I consume is very fresh and rich in flavor, but I feel my body is still lacking something. My drop in weight is beginning to be noticed by my peers and my skin has taken on a bizarre grey coloring. I think all of this stress is weighing too much on my health.

The basement is still serving as a holding pen but I feel it is only a matter of time before someone notices my nightly visits. I overheard some of my classmates speaking of odd sounds coming from the library in the late hours of the night. Soon I may have to relocate.

July 5th, Monday 1751

I reached a new level of frustration! There has been no development in my studies so I decided to dive into the writings of the Macomb and the occult. That is where the infamous wolves of legend and lore come from. I did learn about lycanthropy and its interesting side effects. The reality is...its all true and those who have written the words must have known it to be real. It is all so confusing and surely taking a toll on my wellbeing. Even my fellow students and teachers have taken notice of my rather sickly appearance. They have questioned my good health, I suppose attending a med school is not the best environment to conceal an illness. I cannot deny the truth any longer. It is just as Braun warned, I must feed, and I must hunt to stay alive. Eating beef and kraut with vegetables has only proven I need another source of nourishment. I need the flesh of man...or woman... or I will die, perhaps it is a good thing to die, but Mother would be heartbroken if I were to perish. She has no idea of my condition. I have no other alternative but to feast on the sick or weak. With this realization, I fear the worst is to come, for there is a full moon tonight.

July, 28th Wednesday 1751

A few weeks have passed without innocent, I have fought off the Urge to hunt, but I am almost too weak to put pen to paper. My journal has fallen second to my research, I must find a cure and quickly. There were a few setbacks, for instance, I had to relocate my haven for the night. It seems a few students are using the basement for a project therefore, I have taken residence in the university's storage sheds. I know this is not a very good idea, but it will be adequate for now. The good news is I may have a new approach to the cure. It has been stated in fables that the wolf is susceptible to silver and I did notice the night Dierk was shot he seemed weak and wounded. Balls are usually formed from lead, but sometimes-silver coins are used if the lead is not obtainable. If the projectile was indeed forged from silver then I have found a weakness.

Then again, it is just folklore, but as Professor Haruvo stated, there is always some truth to fabrications. It will be dark soon and with no full moon, tonight will allow me to explore this matter further. I pray it will all end soon. Either my poor health will finish me, or a cure, or...dare I say it...feast. God in heaven, please help me.

August 9th, Monday 1751

My God, what I have done it? Weeks without innocent only to be ruined by a feeble support beam in the shed. It was not strong enough to withhold my strength. The moon last night...the Changing...it was too much to bear. My instincts reached a new level I have never felt before, the hunger, the hunt... I lost control and I fear...no... I know I have caused fatal harm to at least three people. Two men and a woman, I think they were students, and perhaps a teacher. Oh God, they will surely bring the law into this situation. This is making me ill, as a man, I am against any form of harm or violence, but the wolf seems to disagree. The satisfaction of the hunt and the craving for raw flesh and blood prove that I am truly cursed. God had forsaken me and I will surely burn in hell for this. The Urge is getting too strong and the need to feast has drastically increased. The Changing also has become more intense, perhaps it is because I have sustained it for too long. Either way, I must flee this place, somewhere off-campus. Deciding to stay at the university for the summer was a grave mistake. I think it may be time to return home.

September 9th, Thursday 1751

It has been exactly one month since my last entry and I am happy to report there had been no incidents. I returned to Weimar for the rest of the summer and took a well-deserved break. I have experienced the Changing but I was able to lock myself in the stable. Ever since my father was killed in a horse-riding accident, we no longer have any stallions. My mother had sold them all with heartbreak, but she could no longer bear the sight of them. They did go to a good breeder and the money she received from them had put me through school. The stables still stood because my father had invested in good craftsmanship. Thank god for that otherwise they could not withhold my rages.

I had boarded up one area and it seemed to muffle the howls but I fear neighbors still heard my cries in the night. Nevertheless, there had been no killings of late but once again, I find my health declining.

I returned to Gottingen yesterday morning to enroll in the new school year and I am now officially a sophomore. Classes begin next week but I arrived at the university early to continue my research. I have noticed the murders of last month had put the campus on edge but things have gotten back to normal. Still, nothing in my studies has shown any sign of a permanent cure; however, I have been experimenting with small doses of silver nitrate. Placing a few drops in my morning beverages is quite repulsive and nauseating though it seems to keep the wolf within at bay.

There is another pressing matter as well. No stable at the school therefore I have retreated to the library basement. Must I hide in the night forever? Am I doomed to such torture? I will not give up my search to end this.

November 5th, Friday 1751

I have returned home due to the letter I received that Mother has fallen ill. I have been here for almost one week and the dean at the university was kind enough to allow me to make up my studies when I returned. Mother was getting older and it seems she had contracted smallpox. The doctor advised me not to get to close, but I knew there was no human disease that could harm me. I did everything in my power to attend to her needs but I fear she is getting worse and I feel useless. All this time studying medicine and science yet I am still unable to cure my dear mother or myself. My mind and health are not fully functional either, I lack the concentration since I haven't feasted in months. My skin is back to the grayish color and Mother even in her weakened state, still worries about me. I feel to save her I must give her my full attention but to do that I must feed. Dark days indeed, but I will not lose faith, I will still pray even if my God has abandoned me. Tonight hopefully will be a quiet one and I shall increase the doses of silver nitrate. It seems to be helping but for how long? God in heaven, please help us.

November 19th, Friday 1751

Tonight was of unspeakable horror. I had finally decided I needed to hunt. I planned it well, but unfortunately, I made a grave mistake. I looked for stragglers in the streets, or diseased wanders, anyone who was a suitable choice and I found someone. It was a young man who was malodorous and unwashed. He was disgusting, and I could smell the alcohol on him from miles away. For the past few days, I observed his abode and witnessed his abusive ways towards his wife. He was truly a disgrace to any true gentleman, so I chose him. I chose my victim willingly and if I had not been forsaken by God then truly I am now. Premeditated murder has to be one of the foulest sins a man can perform and I ask for forgiveness. It was during the most recent full moon that I decided to feast upon his revolting bones and attacked him while he was in one of his drunken stupors.

He was walking home from the local pub in the dead of night. It was late and I smelled his fear and liquor, I gave in to my instincts, but I did not realize the silver nitrate I have been ingesting was crippling my speed and strength. I attacked the man, but the kill was unsuccessful. The first pounce I had only grazed him, traumatized, he raced across the meadow screaming. My second pounce also failed, as I grew extremely fatigued. I swiped and my claws sliced through his rags but to my surprise, he retaliated. He assaulted me with a brick he had picked up from the ground and struck my face. I continued the chase but he had gotten away. I was just too weak; was I now unable to hunt? If so, I will truly die and that would probably be for best.

The evening had gotten worse as the drunken man alerted the authorities. The incident must have sobered him up enough for them to believe his story so they started a search party and combed the area for a creature only describes as a "Fur beast". They had awoken every person within the town and gained a few volunteers who aided their investigation until late this morning. I locked myself in the stables and made it to the house before anyone could see me; however, I failed at that too, as I entered through the back door, Mother was awake and witnessed my arrival. She saw the blood on my hands and mouth and fainted. I was able to put her back to bed and clean up. Luckily, I did because there was a knock on the door a moment later. It was the local constable asking if I have seen anything the past night. I told him a half-truth that I was taking care of my mother and did not leave the house all night. He was aware of her illness as was the rest of the town and gave us his condolences then departed. I then quickly burned the stained clothes in the fireplace as Mother slept and wondered what she will say when she awakens. I shall pass it off as a bad dream, for there is no explaining this. How could she understand her son is a murderous beast? It would break her heart.

November 21st, Monday 1751

Today is surely the worse day of my entire miserable existence. I have not the words or the reasoning for my dreadful action. My heart is shattered and the guilt has taken hold of me. My dear mother has passed and I am solely to blame. That sweet woman has met death by my own hands. Tears fall down my face as I try to write this entry. After witnessing her son standing in the doorway, covered in someone else's blood was a scene too much for her. She had fainted so I put her to bed but she had awoken early yesterday morning. She woke up terrified and left her room looking for me. I was downstairs by the fire sipping some cognac searching for an explanation, but it was too late for that. She confronted me and again I tried to put her back to bed. She would not have it and told me she overheard the conversation I had had with constable last night about a beast on the loose. My mother is intelligent and quickly put the pieces together. Her first words that morning were "Wilhelm what have you done?" I knew there was not going to be any clarification so I played stupid and told her I had no idea what she rambling on about. It was a bad dream brought on by a fever but she knew better.

She told me I could talk to her and begged me to make my confession to the church and then the authorities. I continued the lie of being ignorant but a mother knows her son, she knew I was hiding something and could even see the torment in my face. She begged me to talk to her, to tell her of the trouble I was in but I could not. I just made her breakfast and we sat in awkward silence for the rest of the day. I hoped it would pass, but I knew my mother, she would pry again. She loved me too much not to. I ignored or changed the subject that was until night came. The damn moon would be full again so I made her tea extra strong in hopes that she would relax and sleep through the night. The search was called off by then and I walked to the stables once again to restrain myself during the Changing. I chained myself up and remembered the howling and trying to break my irons, but then something happened.

Another terrifying occurrence but this one will be forever burnt into my mind. I will never forget these feelings of regret and guilt. Mother had awoken from my howling! Dammit, does that woman ever sleep? Her tea was strong I was sure of it, but somehow she had heard my screams and came to the stables. I remember her staring at me and it was surreal as if I was watching it happen through someone else's eyes. I saw...I remember her standing calling my name, watching me in my wolf form but even then, she recognized her child.

She slowly approached; I could not warn her, tell her to get away! All I felt was rage and hunger, the Urge, the smell, her fear was intoxicating. I heard something snap or bend, and I attacked her.

The mixed emotions I felt must have given me strength beyond the restrictions of the silver. I broke the chains and feasted. I fed on my own mother's corpse and ...and...savored every moment. Even with her sickness, the meat was still rich and good, and yet I felt like I was dying. After that... I remember more...I had escaped... preyed upon a family a few miles away then their livestock, and another family beyond that. The Urge had taken over completely and with the moon so bright and full I had no control. The lack of feasting for so long had caught up with me, it was too much to endure, and I became relentless. My victims from the night before must have been five...no...Seven... my God. Moreover, I left my mother's corpse lying in the stables until this morning. When I returned and found her mangled and eaten, what was left of my soul had died. I will never forgive myself. I wrapped her remains in a blanket and placed her on her bed. I cleaned myself up and called the local doctor. I told him she had past and since he knew of her sickness already he didn't' need to see the body. I told him her dying wish was to be buried on our property next to father. He understood and stated that he would write the legal documentation. He was easily occupied due to the many murders that had taken place by my hand. It seemed my actions as the wolf bought me the time I needed to cover up this tragedy. I buried her this morning in the courtyard.

The rest of that day was agony and the quietness of the house was too much. I could not live like this anymore so I decided to take my own life. I ingested the rest of the nitrate and felt my body and mind slipping. As I lost consciousness, I prayed for God to take me, to forgive me. I gripped my bible and fell to the floor only to awake hours later realizing he had not forgiven me but banned me from the afterlife. I was still alive, sick but alive, the nitrate was not enough to kill me. I tried to hang myself in the stable, then drown myself in the tub, even stab myself in the stomach, all resulted in much pain but not fatal damage. I have been banned from death and this would be my punishment. I was to live forever with the guilt and suffering. It was fitting.

In my dark state of mind, I have decided to flee this house and the university. With the murders and search parties, it would be only a matter of time before they found I was the culprit. There are too many memories here, too many forgotten friends. I have not seen Napes or Kirk in months so they may not miss me either. I will leave tonight and disappear.

October 22nd, Monday 1764

It has been so many years since my last entry, thirteen to be exact. I have been in exile for so long living off animals and unfortunately giving into the Urge. I have feasted on many and fled from town to town, village to village, Word of my killings had spread through the land, and I find myself on the run. It has been a dismal existence, until last night, something had changed, and thus why I have decided to continue my journals.

I had relocated to Hanover and lived with the peasants in Bremen. I was in an alleyway, cold and wet from the rain and had not feasted in weeks. This was because many were alerted of a beast in the area at took heed. Nearly everyone had stayed indoors during the nights and I felt myself getting weak once again. That was until I met a man...well...who at first I thought was man, a Mr. Bonifaz Koch. He found me in a passageway looking pitiful. I was dirty, alone, and hungry. He brought me to his house and that is when I captured his scent. That familiar stench, same as Braun and Dierk but different, it was its own. He was a wolf and I detested that but I could not be rude to someone who had just saved my life. I had met another of my kind and hoped this would be a brief encounter. I took his offer of a warm bed and fire for the night then I would be gone in the morning. He too had a carriage but this was a four-horse and much more lavish then Braun's which I pondered the question, "How do wolves' have some much coin?"

I boarded his coach and he passed me a flask of warm tea and whiskey, I thanked him and we began to talk. He got right to the point, claiming he knew who and what I was. Presenting the experiences I had gone through and comparing them to his own. The loss, the loneliness, running from the law, it was all familiar to him. I told him that I had left school and my studies behind because I was absconding. He claimed to understand and then Mr. Koch questioned me on how many hunts I had done. I lost track after seventeen I told him, and he nodded then asked when I Awakened. I began to tell him the story of my pack with Braun and Dierk. When I finished he chuckled then apologized. His words after were something along the lines of "Sir, that wasn't a pack...that was a...situation." Bonifaz then educated me on how packs truly operate, the calculated hunts, the leaders, the scouted areas, and how they moved in the night. I was very interesting, but still, the guilt burned in me. Even after all these years Mother's death still weighed heavily on my heart. I had contemplated new ways to end myself but had no luck in my attempts.

He brought me to his home, which was a large brick estate, the coach stopped at the front door. I noticed it had stopped raining, and the cool air carried a pleasant scent of wet flowers. We entered a vestibule and a servant brought more drink and a towel to dry my head. I was escorted to the bathroom, where a fresh set of clothes were provided, they fit oddly well, and then I was instructed to meet Mr. Koch in the den. He was sitting by a fire, smoking a pipe, and looked rather posh. A wolf with a pipe, they have to be a farce somewhere in this story. I took a rather comfortable chair and sat, the fire felt good on my bones. Bonifaz proceeded to question my endeavors further, asking me as to how I ended up in such a dreary situation. I told him about my mother and he seemed to understand. His face looked a few years younger than mine did though his eyes projected many more years of wisdom. He asked my place of residence, I spoke of how I fled Weimar with only the clothes on my back, my journal, and what was left of my sanity. He warned that writing down my affairs was dangerous. I told him it was more on my studies and I wasn't that aspired to write about my encounters as a wolf. Rather he believed me or not he still invited me to stay as long as I needed. Breakfast was to be served in the morning and then we would disgust where I was to go from there. I did as he suggested and retired for the night. This morning I found myself refreshed and dry then realized my life had taken another turn. I shall write more tomorrow.

October 23rd, Tuesday 1764

Today was bizarre, to say the least; Bonifaz walked me around the grounds discussing what my next move should be, as in terms to survive. I told him I lived day by day; he spoke to me as a child. He seemed to grow frustrated and said, "That was the typical view of those who had gotten themselves killed". He spoke of how our human side needs to be in control of the wolf. He used the analogy that a zoo is maintained by the keepers while the animals are caged, under control, imagine what chaos would ensue if their circumstances were reversed.

His philosophy made sense, but when the moon was high that was all gone, reality was that I was not in control when the Changing came. He stated I need not to be if I had a plan for what happens after I change. I needed to know where to go after a hunt and anticipate my every move before and after the Changing. I asked how this was possible since while in wolf form we acted on instinct instead of reasoning or logic. He answered by explaining it was like a shepherd herding his sheep only in this situation I happened to be both. Since I possessed the skill to read the sky for the next full moon, I then needed to pick two precise locations, the first being an area for the coming hunt, the second a haven to retreat to afterward. In advance, I would leave a trial, food, or blood, anything that would lure me back to the second location after I fed. With practice, one would recall this ritual from memory during wolf form and return to the designated area safety. I thought this to be preposterous and shook my head in disagreement. Bonifaz begged to differ and claimed he would teach me how to do so.

That afternoon we walked the street of the city and found where the beggars and drunks spent their nights. Again, I found myself nervous and uncomfortable, we were planning more murders, and the thought did not sit well with me. Bonifaz saw my uneasiness and assured me we were hunting, that was all. "A good hunter respects his prey but if we fell into guilt we will starve. It is the way of nature". Nature? There was nothing natural about our state, we were demons, abominations, and cursed by Lucifer himself. There was nothing natural about a Wolfman. Nevertheless, we continued and

Bonifaz showed me the layout of the town. He addressed how many people would be in the pub at this time and what alleyways, streets, and routes they would most likely take while leaving in their drunken states. He also spoke of a short cut out of town as well and I found this ridiculous. In wolf form, I would remember none of this. However, Bonifaz told me, that when the time comes I would indeed recollect and follow him. How did he know that the instant the moon was full we would not try to rip each other apart?

I asked him that and he stated that the more wolfs hunt together the greater the bond, they become organized, trustworthily, become linked in a way he couldn't explain. This may be true on some level. I had read of wolfs in packs form formations to stalk their prey, set traps, and even communicated, but those were real wolves, we were monsters. I followed him for a few blocks, randomly walking up and down the streets. I saw him pause at a corner and then head down a lane. He told me this was the way out of the city, down the alley to the right and under the bridge, there we would follow the river that led into the woods. With our speed, we could cover this distance in under a minute. He tied a piece of wolfsbane to the tree and said it was the key. This was what we needed to get a scent of and follow it out of town. I read wolfsbane was supposed to keep werewolves away, but he stated I had it wrong it was the opposite effect. I watched as he tied it to more to branches and trees along the way and then we headed out of town to his coach. Once aboard he told me the moon would be, half-full and we will not have our full human reasoning. We reached his estate soon afterward I was instructed to rest and reserve my energy. I did not like this; killing again was not right but I needed to feast. I had resisted the Urge successfully before but now with Bonifaz I know I will give into the night. Perhaps it will not be so bad. I again pray to the almighty father for forgiveness.

October 24th, Wednesday 1764

I awoke this morning feeling quite refreshed, but the immoral act I once again committed disgusts me. We preyed on four people last night by that pub Bonifaz showed me the night before. It was grim but our hunt did go as planned though that is no excuse for his constant bragging. His ongoing self-indulgence of how intelligent he is makes physically ill.

The night is still vague in my mind but with each hunt, I seemed to recall more and more details. The pain has decreased with each Changing as well but Bonifaz states that is normal. I remember the wolfsbane and following the trail that led us out of town, though to hunt in such a populated area has me a bit worried. This town is not like back home, it is a small city with many potential witnesses. Luckily, most bystanders were drunk or already passed out from severe intoxication.

After breakfast, Bonifaz wished to revisit the scene of the crime, why, I didn't know nor do I care. I think the idea is in bad taste but he claims it is a good lesson. Since he has provided me with food and shelter, I feel I am in his debt, so I will accompany him but I will not like it. Three men a woman were the causalities of last night; I sincerely hope they did not have children.

October 24th, Wednesday 1764 - Second entry

This afternoon we had visited the street where the hunt took place. Many citizens were lingering around and we were met by the local constable. They had already removed the bodies though many still crowded around as the investigations took place. I was questioned as to where I was and if I saw anything. I quickly stated I was at home that night and Bonifaz of course was my alibi and I his. I still do not understand why we were there until he started to sniff the air. Past scents, he was trying to find which meant he was retracing our steps. He slowly headed off and I followed carefully not to arouse suspicion. I ask him why were taking part in such a strange procedure, he just said it helped him learn. He studied what had become apparent during the hunt and how this helped him lure us back home on the next one. For instance, by picking up faint smells on objects, like fence posts, trees, and even the street itself, he could calculate the time; how much time it took to complete the hunt, and if we were clumsy or efficient. He seemed to be obsessed with his hunts and treated them like historic events. Bonifaz was a man who thought highly of himself. He cherishes his every Changing as if it were a great sporting event. I was sickened by his attitude, murder was not to be celebrated or treasured. It was a crime and we should be incarcerated. He walked to a large tree, sniffed its bark, and told me "This is where we began" then retraced his steps towards the alleyway. Bonifaz stated that the angle of the attack told him we had jumped 30 feet over a small hedge wall and then assailed our second victim. This entire scene happened within 4 seconds and he estimated the time of the whole event was just until 3 minutes. With a smirk, he claimed it was a new record and boosted even more. The Aschloch was competing with himself and proud of it. I had had enough of his overweening and stated I wanted to head home. He seemed disappointed that I was not relishing the moment but complied and we left the streets.

Later that night we retreated to his estate and discussed more over some Scottish whiskey. I still did not quite grasp the significance of revisiting the areas. What did we learn? However, through further inquiry, I did discover some answers but the night started to take a bizarre turn. Bonifaz had documented every hunt he ever executed, down to date and place with estimated times. He showed me ledgers with his so-called accomplishments, like a mighty hunter showing off his stuffed and mounted prizes. I figured he only was arrogant but the following display proved to me that he was truly insane. He motioned me down the hall to a room I had not seen, once we entered the large antechamber what I witnessed next horrify me. It was his collection of human hides, treated and tanned then displayed in small frames. Hundreds of them, lining the walls and he jested that soon he would need a larger room for his trophies. I was sickened by his lack of companion, what he had told me about respecting our prey was a lie!

Bonifaz was a fraud! He stood there, swollen with pride for gross exhibits of people he had murdered. Bonifaz was far beyond disturbed, he was not just a wolf, but also a serial killer. I broke my overdue silence by shouting that I was not impressed and how dare he have such a lack of respect for the dead. His response what that I simply did not understand but I would soon, it was just like Braun all those years ago, always justifying death for a lack of comprehension. No, it was simpler than that, I said we were monsters, uncontrollable cursed individuals, and if it were up to me, I would eradicate our species all from existence. Bonifaz did not favor my outburst, stated I was fatigued, and should retire for the night before I said anything I would regret. I needed rest for tomorrow would be a long day. Why? Would there be another hunt? No, no sleep tonight...even with a moonless sky I still felt nocturnal. The previous feast would keep me satisfied. I shall read his memoirs on his hunts instead. Perhaps I can learn something, a weakness of his, or better, a chance to escape this place.

December 26th, Wednesday 1764

I have not written in months simply because my life here has depressed me in such a manner I did not feel motivated. More hunts had taken place along with Bonifaz dragging me to revisit the scenes. The local town people are now living in fear and hunting has become more of a challenge. Most of them stopped traveling or socializing during the night and feasting is scarce. It has been a cheerless experience and last night was the most horrible, I simply will not forgive that egotistical arschloch or myself for what we had done. On the most sacred day of our lord and savior, we had committed a malicious act that I will never forget.

Yesterday friends of Bonifaz who have come from quite a ways visited us. They were two English gentlemen who spoke German but still with a hint of an accent. Joseph Claremore and Killian Jones, they were colleagues of Bonifaz or so I was told and they thanked us for the invite. I could smell they were of our kind and I became nervous and territorial, my God, I was trying into a common watchdog, another reason to leave this vile place and I would do in time, but now with three against one, I found it hard at the moment. They resided in the spare guest rooms and immediately went to bed. They had arrived early that afternoon and by nightfall planned to be awake and sharp, not uncommon for our kind. In the night, we retreated to the den with some Scottish whiskey while Bonifaz took to his pipe. The aroma was an overwhelming cherry and made me nauseous. Joseph joking stated the pipe was to cover up Bonifaz's stench and with that, he extinguished it in the tray. Thank goodness. We then began to discuss the night's hunt, but I stated it was Christmas, a sacred day and it just would not be appropriate. Killian immediately frowned and I noticed Bonifaz seemed embarrassed by my remark as well. He then outright humiliated me by stating that I was still young, and looked at this with more innocence. Innocence? I was being treated like a child, which was not taken lightly by a man of my education. I wanted to pounce but constrained myself and allowed Killian to continue about the local pub being a target. Bonifaz disagreed and claimed there was a residence just outside of town that would be easier. "It is Christmas and most families will be at home by a fire with their loved ones. It would be easy to find a house, more recluse, and isolated." I told them I would not take part but my stance was only met by laughter. Bonifaz said that tonight was the closest the moon would be to the earth and her power would be more than I have ever experienced thus far. He tried to reverse the argument by debating my point with a spin "It is Christmas, your right Wilhelm, it is a sacred day for Christians, and families, so at this moment are the four of us, not a family?" Killian responded stating that a feast is unusually served on Christmas day so why shouldn't we have one as well. Joseph laughed. These people were awful, Bonifaz reminded me again that I would not be able to resist and would feel better about things in the morning. I disagreed.

We drank more, but it seems alcohol does not have that relaxing effect on me anymore. All I received was a headache but the pain did not damper my focus. I asked Bonifaz about the house's setting and if it were possible to find our way back to the estate. He of course thought about this, and then hesitated to tell me the details. I pressed on and he revealed his devilish plan. The house of interest was to the east and away from the city but in the opposite direction from where we lived. However two more farms where between its location and our estate so we were to take the carriage north, past the house, make camp, and then during the Changing move south. We would assault the inhabitants of the house, and then the scents of the livestock from the two farms should provoke us to move further south. We would take all three residents before sunlight and by the time we finished off the third, we would meet back here. The plan was utterly absurd, we would be only drawing more attention to ourselves. Three families in a single night were not wise! I proposed that we should leave a trail straight back to the house as we did that night with wolfsbane. Bonifaz of course assured me that the authorities would be looking for wild animals instead of humans and that would allow us more time. More time? I knew what he meant; he planned for a blood bath more than a feast. It was not about the hunt for him, just the senseless killing, he loved it, and that made me loathe him even more.

An hour or so had past and nightfall was approaching so we boarded his coach and rode for miles. The ride was cold of course, but the scenery was beautiful. The setting sun reflecting off the snow brought a nice calm to the night. Hence it is just as they say; "It is always quietest before the storm". I still was completely against this idea. I hated myself more with every moment of the sinking sun; I tried justifying this decision in my mind. I was not sure if it was the wolf speaking or I was just trying to rationalize for the sake of my sanity, nevertheless, the night would soon be upon us and I needed to be ready.

We reached the camp spot, it was covered in trees and in the distance, and we could eye the house. Smoke was billowing out the chimney and I could see shadows inside by the light of the fireplace. My nerves were getting the best of me and so were the Urges. I noticed Killian and Joseph; they were excited as the moon started to show itself. It was quick and I then remembered the Changing. Though now I remember it all, perhaps because I have changed so many times before that I was growing accustomed to it. I did not like it! It was as a part of my soul was cursed to remember all the violence and pain and yet something else. It was the first time I hunted with an actual pack, it was execrating. Our tactics were all instinctual as if we were being instructed by a higher power. We were so organized, so calculated, we took the house with such speed and strength that is was over in a matter of minutes. Bonifaz was the first in because naturally, he had to lead the charge. Joseph entered from the window, Killian, and I and waited for the family to be flushed out. They had split up in a panic and we had surrounded them. I attacked the mother first and Killian and Joseph took the man of the establishment.

There were more adults, perhaps aunts, uncles, or random relatives and I pursued one through what I remember as being the kitchen then the storage room. I ripped the door off the wall without realizing its weight. It was solid oak but I was more aggressive than ever and only saw these poor people as only food, as a butcher sees his cow or a lion his prey. They served one purpose, which was to feed us. I grabbed the man by his face, carried him away from the house, his throat was soft and easily ripped out along with his neck bone. The flesh was invigorating and I howled in satisfaction.

The rest of the night however is only a blur. That was usual so I assumed we must have completed Bonifaz's plan and attacked the local farms. I vaguely remember eating a sheep and crossing a large open field before returning home. This morning I found myself on the divan. I felt well rested, that was until I heard the sounds of clanging silverware and laughter. I arose and entered the kitchen where I saw the three maniacs enjoying themselves a little too much. Bonifaz saw me enter the room and raised his glass, which was filled with a Northern Harvest Rye, it displayed his lack of any intellectual awareness. One does not drink such liquor in the morning hours, it's considered uncouth. He then commented on how I could not endure a long night of hunting as best as they could. Joseph smirked yet came to my defense as he declared I performed very well and my speed was most impressive. Getting a compliment like that was like being encouraged by a serial killer. I remained silent and sat by the fire as Bonifaz proceeded to boast about how his plan succeeded more than he even anticipated thus proving that he was a master pack hunter. He carried on as to how we were a new beginning and with his experience, he could lead us onto great hunts with never the worry of finding prey again.

His speech was offensive, and his bragging along with the high opinion of himself was just as equally distasteful. Regardless of the celebration around me, I could not forget the truth. We had killed a family on Christmas night. It was horrible and if I had enough silver nitrate, I swear at this moment I would inject all of us with it. These people were downright evil and I once again found myself in league with the foulness but what could I do? The disaster we constructed surely caused attention but if I were to leave now, the harsh winter outside would be my demise. For now, this place was the only shelter I have, so I shall pray… pray for forgiveness and pray to forget this day.

December 27th, Tuesday 1764

I knew it; I knew eventually that we would attract attention to ourselves. A couple of local constables visited us this afternoon. I welcomed them in and desperately wanted to tell them everything. I just wanted this to end, but just like before I knew they would not believe my story. I tried to keep my composure no matter how hard it was. I did notice Bonifaz seemed nervous and frightened by their questions. His anxiousness I found amusing and how they did not see through his guilty face and mannerisms are beyond me, he was truly terrified. It was almost pathetic and his fear seemed to spread as well. Joseph was also uneasy and sat in silence, Killian followed. I found myself doing most of the talking with them, and discovered it was merely a courtesy call. One of the constables introduced himself as Chief Hoffmann and stated that a family in the east had been attacked by what seemed like a pack of rabid wolfs. I acted shocked and then we were asked if we had seen or heard anything in the past few nights. I stated no and told them we would say a prayer for the family. My performance was more believable than the three fools, so I took control of the incident, which was until Bonifaz began to ask bizarre and juvenile questions. He wanted to know how bad the bodies had been ripped apart and if there were any survivors. The constable was disturbed by his insensitivity and he relayed to me a confused look. I merely shook my head and tried to dismiss his ignorance but he continued about how a mere

MY WOLF WITHIN 1750-1783

wolf could not do that much damage and the authorities should further their investigation.

This is when things started to unravel; the constable began getting suspicious and continued his questions. Bonifaz was also getting nervous and I could smell his guilt so I tried to defuse the situation. I told Hoffmann my friend had participated in a Christmas celebration and took on to much Rye and cigars. The constable did not have faith in my words and it was that exact moment I realized he knew something. His scent changed and the small glare in his eye gave him away. Hoffmann was an older gentleman with experience, he knew the signs of a guilty suspect, and Bonifaz was projecting one perfectly. I keep calm and assured him that my friend would be going to bed soon, he only and stated, "Be sure that he does." then bid us a goodnight. I closed the door and was relieved but I knew this was not the end of the Chief. Joseph looked relieved and Killian snickered like a childish five-year-old who had just got away with stealing some sweets from the local candy store.

Bonifaz's fear disappeared and his arrogance returned while guaranteeing us we had nothing to worry about. The man was ...annoying. I told him he was a fool and that we should hold off on the hunting. They protested of course and I warned them that Hoffmann knew we were up to something. My warning was countered with laughs and accusations of paranoia. Killian's ignorance was astonishing. He stated I need not be afraid because they were looking for a pack of rabid wolfs instead of us. I could only roll my eyes at his statement. I knew the constable would be watching us; one simple mistake would put us in jeopardy. Oh, I wish I could just leave these fools but not with the whole town on edge. I will have no other choice but to wait and see what the future holds.

December 29th, Saturday 1764

Today Bonifaz purposed we partake in a traditional hunt to bring in the New Year. I was repulsed, this all seemed too familiar, and now I officially hated New Year's Eve. He proclaimed that he had heard of a local party taking place on Eve and that afterward the streets would be loaded with drunken fools for our pickings. I told him that would be a bad idea; to hunt in crowded streets was too risky. However, the thought of the feasting made my mouth water and I did crave the flesh again. I reminded them of Hoffmann along with the rest of the authorities. Most likely, they would be patrolling the streets and certainly be armed. Again, my counsel was met with their drunken slurs and they protested with jokes, making me the butt of most of them. I was used to the mocking by now and knew my warnings fell upon deaf ears, even though it was the most drastic move on our part. I could feel with every fiber of my being that it was not going to end well.

January 1st, Tuesday 1765

I write this with much blood hands and my mind shaken. We are now in grave danger due to the idiocy of Bonifaz's plans. Last night was debauchery after deciding to follow through with his proposal for the New Year's Eve hunt. Though I was at my ends with this entire ordeal, I still needed to feast so I participated. Bonifaz had stated that the town hall would be the staging area where there was a gathering taking place. The entire town attended, my nerves were thin. I envisioned multiply scenarios of how this could go wrong, having the entire town spotting us, knowing of our existence, I could see masses of angry villagers with torches and muskets hunting us in the woods. Oh, how I wished I stayed home.

We attended the party and I danced with a few women who seemed to fancy me especially Ms. Lauren. She was beautiful, with blond locks, a warm smile, and seemed to value my company for most of the night. I enjoyed her presence very much. Then that supercilious ass Bonifaz approached us and I had to excuse myself. I thought about how in my current state I could never court such a woman. How could I proclaim my intentions while infected with this curse? It best to not be involved but I found it difficult to forget her.

Just before midnight we had left the party unnoticed and waited for the attendees to leave. The moon was exceptionally vivid; the cool air seemed to numb our sense of smell, but not our appetites. After a few hours of watching and picking our prey, Killian stopped a couple leaving the hall. They had exited through the back and chose a trail to follow, not the smartest decision. That path would lead them right through the quad of the old school and away from the public eye.

For once, I agreed with the pack, they would be a good choice. Then through our inexperience for awareness, we were noticed. How long I was not exactly sure and I will rectify soon, but as the night went on, we had successfully attacked the couple. During the feast, I heard musket fire and I saw Killian drop to a knee. He had been shot. I was not aware of it at the time, but looking back I know the constable and his men had spotted and us.

They had been on patrol that night as I assumed and must have witnessed us leaving the party. It was as I had warned them, after the first shot I remember shouting, growling, and then we separated. I think Joseph might even have attacked someone as more shots rang out, and then I retreated here, home. I was the last to return as I remember being awoken in the basement by noise and then the breaking of the door. I heard another musket discharge and came upstairs. There I was confronted by Hoffmann along with five other men armed, all shouting at me. To my left was Killian on the couch, still bleeding and lifeless. They had shot him while he was in wolf form and tracked him back here. Those fools, they had all came back to the house and lead Hoffmann right to us. Killian was dead though, which means they waited until he changed back to human form and killed him. They had killed a wounded and unarmed man. In a rage, Bonifaz changed again as did Joseph and I followed. I do not remember anything after that until we awoke again in the front room, bloodied and beaten with five corpses and Killian surrounding us. Blood smeared on the walls, floor, and ceiling. Damaged furniture and broken body parts littered the area. The hellish scene would have made the strongest men weak and sick, but I had been used to the blood. I felt disgusted that I had grown accustomed to such violence. Joseph was sitting on the couch in shock when I woke on the floor. I moved to a chair and made eye contact, but he seemed to be in disbelief and a then voice came from the back. It was Bonifaz; oh, I wished at that moment that it were he and not Killian who had been killed. He stated he was glad I was up and ok, and gave me a glass of brandy. I refuse to drink it, I told him at the moment we needed to leave. He shook his head, "We must clean this place up". I reminded him that the noise from last night's battle would have surely alerted the neighbors, but he refused to believe me, He was also in shock and tried to find rational ties in his twisted mind to stay here. I told him we had gone too far, and his plan for New Years had failed miserably. He argued that we did not fail, and it was only Hoffmann who had pressured us into this; we were merely defending ourselves. He was beyond his normal level of disillusions. I have had enough and as I took my first step towards the broken door where I was quickly confronted by Joseph and Bonifaz, warning me that I could never leave.

I was told that I could not be trusted and even accused of telling Hoffmann about our pack. That idea was obscure, but I had become their scapegoat for Bonifaz's failure. I was not scared of their threats and made my move towards the door, but again met with overwhelming force. They had beaten me well and I quickly retreated to my room afterward. My face battered and my left eye had been swollen shut. I have no permanent injuries by my hands are inflamed and I find it hard to hold my quill. My legs have gotten the worst of it. They have not broken any bones, perhaps due to the wolf blood that runs through me, but I am in great pain and it is hard to walk, I have no idea how I am to escape this place now, and in my current condition, I cannot hunt with the others. Perhaps they will let me starve and I am sure more will come looking for us soon. I have only dark days to look ahead for.

April 16th, Thursday 1778

Thirteen years have passed, thirteen atrocious agonizing years that I have been bounded in chains, still here, still at Bonifaz's estate. Only recently have I managed to break my restraints. Those fools are too stupid to realize that metal even grows weak against a wolf's continued abuse. The manacles finally twisted and broke allowing me to return to my room upstairs. I have found my journal and write this entry after over a decade of being a pet, fed scraps, and not allowed to hunt. They have barely kept me alive, too weak to escape, and too frail to fight them both. I can only bide my time for now and continue to be their prisoner.

I remember that night so many years ago, that night after we had a good hunt nearly fifty miles always from the estate. I remember that we had hunted so many times that people started fleeing and soon the city became vacant. We should relocate I kept telling them, but Bonifaz refused to leave this horrible place. I remember after the night Killian was killed, we retaliated in kind against Chief Hoffmann and his men. Without any constables, the people started taking heed. The warning and whispers of the townsfolk, mentions of monsters and wolf-like demons were on the loose, and they were not wrong. People became reclusive and in time, the local events and festivals disappeared. Hunting became more difficult so we had to stretch out our territory until it was nearly impossible to return before sunrise. Joseph kept his loyalties to Bonifaz for many years; he was a coward and did not dare to leave. He would rather endure the madness then make a stand, but fear is not fed by reasoning.

It was a summer night, hot and I remember taking part in a hunt that nearly exhausted us. We had changed back to our human forms before returning home. The morning came quickly and we found ourselves thirteen miles away from the estate. We walked back in the hot sun, without water, covered in blood. Fatigued and dehydrated we were easily noticed by many townsfolk. It was not long after that they had figured out we were behind the missing and the murdered. Our bizarre behavior aroused great suspicion. As the days went by people started to view us strangely, they were frowning upon our mere presence and even Ms. Lauren distanced herself. One afternoon as she was coming home from her place of work, I smiled and gestured a wave, it was returned with an uncomfortable gaze and an expression of fear. She broke eye contact with me and ran into her home. From then on, it would be only a matter of time before we would be run out of town, and I was almost correct.

Two nights later, a new constable, Chief Gorwin Demak, along with the rest of the towns' people, approached us. They came to our doorstep and threaten to chase out of town if we did not leave immediately. Bonifaz of course was furious and made a few threats of his own and Demak almost took him into custody. I again defused the situation as Joseph just sat on the porch like a timorous child. I promised them we would be leaving in the next few days if no trouble was to start; Demak agreed that that was best and then ordered the mob to return to their homes. It was a narrow escape, but then Bonifaz lashed out at me and called me a coward. He insisted we attack them, that we could own this city by making the residents fear us. I disagreed stating we were outnumbered and the element of surprise was gone, they knew about us. I turned to go upstairs, proclaiming my resignation from the pack. Then I recall Joseph hitting me over the head with something large and I fell unconscious. When I awoke I was in chains and down in the cellar. I have no knowledge of what has taken place in the past thirteen years but I am quite sure it is bleak. Though now I am free, I'll be able to steal food when I have the chance, for now, I stay down here and continue to be their prison until I gain my strength, then may God help the both of them.

May 2nd, Sunday 1778

I still wait patiently in the cellar for any chance for flight. I am keeping the deception of remaining weak, and their prisoner successfully. I overheard Bonifaz speak of a hunt tonight in Leipzig, which is approximately 22 miles from the estate. If they chose to do this, they will surely be gone for the entire night. It will be the perfect time to attempt my escape. The bars on my shackles are rotten and rusted so I should be able to remove them from my hands. This will allow me access to the view from the cellar window. If the moon is full tonight, I will change and have enough strength to break free from my cage.

I have rationed some food by hiding it under piles of hay they had provided me for a bed. The meat is somewhat rancid but should supply enough nutrients. I will reserve my energy and once they leave, I will make an effort to finally escape this hell.

May 3rd, Monday 1778

Last night did not go as well as I had hoped. I realized I am still far too weak for any permanent escape. I would not survive a journey far enough away from those two. They would track me so I must change my strategy and wait a while longer. After locked away for thirteen years what are a few more months? Summer will be upon us soon, the warmer weather should allow me to flee this place easier.

After Bonifaz and Joseph left the estate last night, I waited about a half-hour and executed make my escape. I was right, the moon was full and I could feel the urge again, I quickly left my chains and ran to the window. There I saw the moonlight for the first time in years and bathed in its glory and bright light. The air was cool and refreshing and I could feel the Changing happen, I focused, trying not for the rage to overtake me. I remember consuming the stockpile of food and feeling full but unsatisfied, the doors... I broke through them to the upstairs and out the back way but I was still weak. It drained me quickly and in my fatigued state, I grew sluggish. My sense of smell seemed to be unaffected and I remember hunting, but only feasting on cattle roaming the pasture. I then woke in the wheat field and I tried to keep the idea of not wondering to far, but my instincts still took over. With experience, I was now able to stay conscious and in control while in wolf form. The weather shifted, the moon became clouded, and its crescent shape allowed me to retain a few of my human rationalities as the Changing took place.

The second time I awoke it was still night, the sun had not risen yet which was good. I figured I would be able to retreat to my prison before Bonifaz and Joseph returned so I started my walk through the woods and towards the town. I did have cattle blood on me but it was better than the alternative. I noticed I had traveled much farther than I had anticipated, my instincts blindly lead me to the nearest feeding source, which was logical since I have not hunted in so long. The cattle were the source and since the moon was weak, I only held form for a short time. This made me reach the conclusion that if Bonifaz and Joseph were out here and far from home, they might not hold their form either. It would take quite some time to return, and they were in much better shape than I was so I could not hesitate.

As I made it back to the town, the sight awed me, thirteen years had indeed passed, but for the city, it seemed more like twenty. I roamed through it quickly and failed to see any town residents. There were a few shadows behind curtains in homes, but other than that, the town seemed bare. I felt discouraged as I walked more through the desolate and soulless streets. The church had been burned down and the town hall seemed like it had been pillaged. I was reminded of the News Year's party so many years ago, the place where I had danced with Ms. Lauren for the first time. I wondered where she was, or what had happened to her. I ran to her home and found it in shambles; the doors had been kicked in. The sight filled me with rage, for if Bonifaz had brought harm to her I would surely be the bringer of his demised. I entered but only found small remains of something or someone. I prayed it was not Ms. Lauren, and that she somehow escape this hell. Without proof, I will never surely know, but my heart tells me otherwise. Bonifaz your days are numbered.

I left her establishment and searched the town further, more houses were ruined, the barns were destroyed, and there was freed livestock in the streets with bodies left on porches to rot. My god, this place has fallen, fallen to Bonifaz and Joseph's will. How could only two wolves bring so much destruction? They had taken this place and drained it to the point where they needed to feed elsewhere.

I would be feeding on livestock again for that was the only source of food that remained. This entire experience left me defeated, nothing in this town could fully regain my strength. I retreated to my cage, praying, but my faith is dwindling.

August 21st, Friday 1778

I have been too weak to write of late. Three more months have gone by and it seems my plans for escape during this summer are becoming less feasible. I had continued to leave in the night but feasting on cattle has become scarce and I am left to eat rats and snakes. I may have smelled a few of the remaining residents lingering in the town, but if so, they hide well. I would assume Bonifaz is too obtuse to know they still reside here. I remember the house, yellow and stained by weather, nearly three lots away. I saw shadows there. If I could hunt, feast there, I might be able to gain enough strength to escape, but I could barely make this entry let alone fight for food. I have lost weight and the Changing is not that intense anymore. Joseph still brings me scraps, but since they are hunting so far out, it is harder and harder to carry more food back home. I begged them to kill me, but they refused and said I needed to learn. I fear my fate will be living my last few days in this barred enclosure.

August 23rd, Sunday 1778

Last night as I rested on the cold hay covered floor and prepared for my death, I heard a voice come from upstairs. I listened carefully, but I could not place it. It was clear and strong, definitely a male with a deep tone. I did not recognize it at all. Was it someone new? Perhaps new residents had come, or had those two idiots finally fled this place? I hope that a new constable had killed them, but my luck was not that reliable. I wanted to yell but my voice was to dry, then I heard Bonifaz and Joseph and became distraught. They were in conversation with this new person, my God had they found another wolf? Laughter came, I sniffed the air and recognized two scents and an unknown third, but it carried a familiar aroma. My assumption was true, they had meant another of our kind, but there were only three. Three was considered minimal for a pack, but I was still too weak to face them. They had filled the void I had left and perhaps now they could put me out of my misery, I served no purpose to them anymore.

November 1st, Saturday 1778

Today was a welcoming turn of events. The morning seemed to change my position within this scenario of surrendering. I heard the stranger's voice again, but it was loud clearer than before, and footsteps approached my cage. I was so weak I did not even sit up. I was out of breath and my head was pounding. I had still gone through the Changing once every few weeks, but I became so weak during the process that I exhausted myself and fainted, all to wake up and to do it again. Today however was different, when I heard that voice; I opened my eyes and saw then biggest human figure I had ever seen. He stood at least 6'3 and perhaps just over 250 pounds. The large figure was standing at my cage door and quite befuddled. I heard him say my name, "Wilhelm...this is Wilhelm isn't it?" I then saw Bonifaz standing in his shadow and he responded by telling this man I was being punished. The stranger stated he had been told I had died and asked why he was being deceived. Bonifaz stated he would not understand and this was the way of *his* pack. I chuckled at his words and then the door flew open. I was not sure as to who had spoken next, but I felt myself being pulled up, the rusty manacles scrapped my wrists as they freed me and I was carried. I was put on the couch upstairs and the dust caused me to cough. My bones were aching, but that couch brought some comfort. The words "Brother your safe now" echoed in my ears and I could see the large man handing me something, food, fresh food that smelled incredible. I ate without hesitating. If the food was poisoned so be it, I was famished. While I ate, I heard chuckling. Bonifaz's high pitch voice pierced the silence as he protested but there were low growls and then silence.

As I devoured my meal, my strength seemed to return rather quickly, I filled my stomach to fast and I started to feel sick but it was too good to stop. I continued to eat like a mindless beast. I could feel my body absorb the protein and instantly my eyes cleared, my breathing hardened and my ears became more sensitive. All my senses seemed to be all coming back and at an alarming rate. If this continued, I could leave this place tonight.

The large man extended his hand, introduced himself as Kristoph, and stated he was indeed a wolf. I ignored him and continued to feast as he went on about his story. During a mutual hunt, he had met Bonifaz and Joseph by capturing their scent. He hoped they were not territorial but by his size, even if those two buffoons were defensive of their surroundings, they were no threat to this Kristoph. I finally ceased eating and thanked him for his kindness; he nodded and then scolded the two idiots. He stated this was no way to treat a brother and they should be banned from the region. Joseph of course was submissive and Bonifaz tried to explain what had happened over the years. He blamed me for being incompetent, and that I posed a threat to their survival. I was the reason that the town had turned on them and why they had to slaughter everyone for survival. His words confirmed that Ms. Lauren was now certainly deceased and by his hand. In my anger, I lunged at Bonifaz but my weakness still limited me and I retreated to the couch. Kristoph told me to rest and in the morning, they would discuss the issue further, and then insisted I was to reside on the couch and never return to that cage.

I did just that as the three hunted that night. They returned earlier than I expected and I took that to mean they might have found a better hunting ground. We all retired early. For tomorrow, we were to discuss our next move. I had a feeling this Kristoph will bring many changes in our current state of affairs. He does seem to be level headed and does not care for Bonifaz anymore then I do. Perhaps Kristoph is the ally I need, though I still do not trust him. Therefore, as long as he does not get in my way of avenging Ms. Lauren, we shall get along fine.

November 2nd, Monday 1778

Tonight the four of us discussed what our next intentions would be. Joseph of course was again the submissive one but I must admit his loyalty towards Bonifaz was impressive. Kristoph on the other hand seemed to be the opposite and stated his views. I wanted to leave, but my revenge towards Bonifaz seemed to be my new priority. I also knew he would only try to hunt me down if I were to flee on my own. Being in a weakened state I just listened and made myself look worse than I felt. I wanted Bonifaz to think I was pathetic. It would give me more of an advantage when I decided to kill him. He opened the meeting by addressing our current situation. He admitted that Joseph and he had indeed chased away or preyed upon the entire down. Bonifaz claimed that because of this it was now desolate and empty. I knew differently, there were still survivors and they were intelligent. They knew Bonifaz was around and that he hunted at night. Even with our hunts unpredictable to the normal eye, someone smart enough would eventually make the connection between the full moon and our pack. Bonifaz continued and what he announced changed everything. He confessed why he could not leave this city. It was because the land possessed a rich deposit of ore. He was planning to retrieve a fortune, but once word reached the other cities, people would come from all over. So by traumatizing the locals, and performing bloody massacres, rumors would spread that, the city was cursed, keeping outsiders too frightened to come here. It made sense; Bonifaz was sitting on a gold mine, probably with the original owners murdered by his hand so he could conveniently hold the deed.

It would be legal, but the problem was these fables of wolfs were now true, thus scaring all our local and potential food away. No one was coming, at least not until the folklore had died down and we would starve by then. Kristoph proclaimed himself as an experienced traveler, thus had seen this type of greed destroy packs in the past. He agreed with me that we move on and search for better hunting grounds. Bonifaz refused and that cowardice Joseph supported him. It seemed to be a stalemate so I suggested that we split up and head north, but Kristoph told me I would never survive alone in my state and he wished to go elsewhere. He wanted to venture across the sea, to a faraway land, it sounded like a myth. I respected his vision but hoped he would not depart for that would only reverse things. If he was to leave I would find myself right back in that cage. I placed my concern about this and he claimed he would not leave me alone with the two of them until I healed properly. I thanked him but we remained at a stalemate. I purposed a solution; give me two weeks to make a full recovery, after that, I would stay with the pack on the condition that we raided the mines. It would be in Bonifaz's favor of a 60-40 split and since he still held the deed, he could return later on his own for more ore if he wished. Once I got my share, I would then finally be free of them and this city. They contemplated the idea and by my surprise, an agreement was reached. In two weeks we were to clean out the gold, take our shares, and disband. What I failed to tell them was that once I received my share I would seek my revenge and kill Bonifaz. If Kristoph wished to help he was welcome too, if not his share would be enough to finance his trip. (The place he speaks of across the Atlantic does sound fascinating.) This gold could allow me to obtain a very secure establishment somewhere far way and new. It was a fine plan and I had initiated the first step. If all goes well I shall be rich and avenge Ms. Lauren's death very soon.

November 17th, Tuesday 1778

The time had come, my health has fully been restored I can hunt on my own again. Kristoph has been a great help towards my recovery and I am in his debt. Bonifaz of course grumbled and complained the entire time; he has the patience of an infant and the intelligence of yak, though that no longer matters. This afternoon we reviewed our plan. I assured everyone I was well and we needed to move as soon as possible. The moon tonight would not rise, for the overcast during the day was thick. There would be no Changing this evening, which would work out well for us. The night before we had feasted and our stomachs were still full. (Bonifaz of course wanted to go easy and prey upon an orphanage. I found this dishonorable and Kristoph agreed, we dismissed that idea and decided to hunt due north. About five miles out of the city there were rumors of bandits causing problems and we investigated. We found them by posing as weary travelers. We let them kidnap us and were brought back to their camp. During the night, we...let us say, turned the tide in our favor. We returned unseen and awoke this morning with full bellies.)

Recently I have been getting the tools ready for the job but I feel an unsettling intuition in the pit of my stomach. Bonifaz could not be trusted, but I felt he would not dare defy the both of us. Kristoph alone had the size of an ox and the submissive Joseph was not a threat. The feeling went away as I concentrated on the job at hand and loaded up the cart with pickaxes and hammers. Bonifaz stated that inside the mine, there was ore already processed and ingots of gold had been made. Naturally, I did not believe him; I did not believe any word that spilled from his vile mouth, so I ready myself for any deception.

We had loaded up the cart, the horses, and headed to the mine just as the sunset. It was not too far of a ride but all uphill. The horses had no problem getting there, and once we reached our destination Bonifaz informed us that the rest of the journey would be on foot. Kristoph carried the largest bag of equipment over his shoulder as I brought the shovels and chain breaker. Bonifaz held a large bag and assisted Joseph with his things. In a few minutes, we had reached the mine. I saw a small entrance carved into the side of a mountain. I lit a torch to light the way and entered. It looked like it had been abandoned for many years and if there was a fortune in there, I doubt anyone was left alive to know its whereabouts.

The air was dry and dusty; Kristoph went in first followed by Bonifaz then Joseph and I covered the rear. I did not trust those fools so if they planned anything I would be closest to the exit. The mine was fairly large inside with rusty carts and broken railway tracks. Further down we saw many tunnels with large open areas and more equipment, surrounded by a few tables and chairs. I lit more torches on the walls and that feeling of claustrophobia seemed to disappear. Bonifaz laid a map on one of the dirty workbenches and pointed to the west corridor. He claimed the golden ingots were down in the left tunnel. He was not sure how many were there but even if found one, between the four us we would be rich men.

Kristoph spotted a wheeled cart near and informed us to load it with only half of its maximum weight, then take two bars apiece and place them in our coat pockets. This way if something was to happened that caused us to split up we still had a portion on our person. Bonifaz asked if I planned any unexpected proceedings and I ignored his outburst. I only carried on further down the mine and kept to the right but I noticed another opened area a few feet away. In the back, a cage with wooden structures fashioned to the rock. They were large shelves nailed together and the entire apparatus looked rather new. Soot seemed to have covered the shelves and I could not see what lied atop of them. We entered the area, reached the cage, but its door was wrapped with a rusty chain and lock. Kristoph examined it and swung the pickaxe breaking it easily; the door swung inward and he made Bonifaz enter first. He did eagerly and ran to the shelves; there was a stacked pile of ingots waiting for us. (Several of them and made from pure gold.) Bonifaz held one up to the burning torch and it glistened in the light. I could not believe it, he told the truth and we began to laugh. We cackled like lunatics and for a few seconds, I almost had forgotten the past thirteen 13 years of hell. I remember laughing hard and feeling joy. He passed me an ingot, and for that moment, I had forgiven Bonifaz and Joseph for keeping locked away in that basement. Forgave them for Ms. Lauren, I would gladly take my share for compilation and be done with both of them. I saw that this could not only give me a new start but also allow me to return to the university and revert to finding a cure for this curse.

Kristoph fetched the wheel cart and brought it up to the cage. We loaded it quickly counting 25 bars and 2 nuggets. I told them Kristoph and I would take a nugget each and they could have the extra bar. They agreed happily as I took two bars myself and placed them in my pockets. Their weight was cumbersome, but I did not mind, it was the therapy for all tribulations. We headed back and I brought up the rear while Kristoph was in front of me with his cart. Bonifaz and Joseph took point then we rested for a minute in the area where we reviewed the map. I heard Joseph say he was going to spend his share on whiskey and woman, I figured that. He did not have the mind to invest in new endeavors or ideas and within months, he would be back in poverty.

A few moments later we started to move again and that is when I recall a scent, something odd, something I did not recognize, but it was strong. It was the mixture of fear and hate and Kristoph slowed his pace. I asked him what was wrong; he just stated there was light ahead. I could see a hint of it. It was sunlight; our quest had taken all night. I squinted but could not see the exit ahead, yet the smell had gotten stronger. Suddenly I heard a deafening roar and then stone and dust from above fell upon me. The ceiling collapsed right in front of me cutting off my route. It went completely dark and I separated from Kristoph and the rest. I heard shouting and tried to dig my way out but felt another tremor. I became still and the vibrations seemed to cease. Once the dust settled, I wiped the dirt from my face with my handkerchief and ran back to the opening. To my horror it was closed, the cave-in had sealed my fate. I shouted but only hear distant muffled voices respond to my cries. I screamed again and tried to dig myself out once more. Again, the voices were distance, I quickly removed pounds of rock and stone, but my efforts were in vain, I was trapped.

That was four hours ago. I sit here with only a small candle I found as my light. Fortunately, I brought my rucksack with water, food, and my journal. I did search for tools and found a pickaxe, for the past two hours I have been digging with no success. Soon I will sleep but now I pray that this is just a temporary setback. I know Bonifaz was behind it somehow and that thought makes me restless, all I can do is try to escape this new prison or wish to be rescued. At this moment, I do not see either one occurring presently.

November 19th, Thursday 1778

Two days have passed since my last entry and I think I have made progress. I have dug into the rock and it seems I have gotten further but still no sign of daylight. The air is dank and the dust is making it difficult to breathe. By rationing my food, I am able to save a few more days worth. It is enough to keep my strength up for now, but if I do not feast soon I will not have enough energy to carry on.

November 21st, Saturday 1778

I have burrowed through more stone but another cave-in occurred, resulting in an injury to my arm. The wound is not bad though it has caused me to cease for the day. Still no sign of daylight or fresh air so I fear there is only more rock in my way. I did search for another exit or even a break in the stone somewhere else but the mine seems to have only one entry. My water supply is getting low; I only have a few days left. Tomorrow I will search again and pray for a release from this place.

November 22nd, Sunday 1778

My prayers have been answered, this morning or afternoon, it is hard to tell in the darkness. I heard a familiar voice call to me. It was Kristoph and it was good to hear him. He shouted through the rocks for me not to speak in fear of taking up to much oxygen, so I reverted to the use of Morris code. I tapped out my plan for the both of us to dig towards each it at different intervals. This would avoid another cave-in, but Kristoph stated that it was unlikely to occur because the rock formation and the supports remained intact. Still, we proceeded with caution and dug relentlessly. I worked this morning into the early afternoon and he continued into the night. I gained a sense of time by him calling it out every three hours. It had been a long day but I will break out of this situation soon.

November 24th, Tuesday 1778

I am free! After a huge amount of endless digging, I finally broke free from my dusty grave. As the rocks crumbled from Kristoph's efforts, I could see the crack of daylight. I climbed through the hole and felt a hand grab my wrist and pull me through. The light did hurt my sensitive eyes, but they adapted quicker than I expected. I leaned up against the outer support beam and caught my breath, which again was not that hard to do. This wolf blood, disease, curse, whatever it was, did have its advantages when it came to physical abilities. As my eyes recovered from three days of complete darkness, I saw my friend standing there with a grin on his face, hands dirty, and a wound on his head. The bandage mostly covered the back of his skull and I asked him what had happened. He told me when the collapse had occurred, he had gotten out in time but tried to see if I have survived. As he turned back, something struck on the head. He awoke the next day and noticed the gold cart was gone and so were Bonifaz and Joseph. I cursed those two for their betrayal but Kristoph insisted they had not caused his injury though took advantage of the situation. They had left us for dead and escaped with the gold. He looked discourage until I removed the ingot from my trench coat pocket and handed it to him. He was grateful as I told him half of it was payment for saving my life and the other half would be for helping me retrieve the rest from Bonifaz.

Kristoph was more forgiving than I was and stated if they did flee with the gold we should let them be. Perhaps, but he was not the one who had been chained up for thirteen years. He also had not lost someone by the hands of those maniacs, so I disagreed. (Strange that in the presence of gold, one can have a false sense of forgiveness, but in its absence, retorted back to bitterness.) I told him they both lacked the imagination to do anything intelligent with the gold. Knowing Bonifaz, he returned to his estate and was boasting to Joseph, he was too much of a coward to explored or move on. He also feared others of our kind, except Joseph because he was a sniveling dolt. I claimed that if they thought we both perished in the accident we could take them by surprise. He was apprehensive but with some persuasion, Kristoph agreed. The terms were he was to receive payment upon assisting me with my revenge, and then we were to dissolve our partnership and go our ways. We settled the accord with a handshake and a promise. Tonight we shall bring hell an upon the Koch estate.

November 25th, Wednesday 1778

I write this, covered in the blood, standing in the middle of the main hall inside the Koch estate. I regret the crimson stains are not from the wounds of my enemies Joseph or Bonifaz himself, but only the local humans who have sought my harm. Our plan was almost executed perfectly until a few unexpected constables accompanied by more angry townsmen called upon the front door. A simple matter of bad timing mixed with an unfortunate turn of events and brought on by sheer stupidity and greed, resulted in a massacre with casualties on both sides. (Joseph... Joseph you are an idiot of unmeasured proportions.)

Last night Kristoph and I reached the courtyard of Bonifaz's estate just as it had become dark, the clouds parted as they do with a full moon and we began the Changing. It was bright and magnificent, giving us such clarity and focus. I remember everything, the yard, the door, and the smell of fear, hatred, hunger, and then the enemy. I knew we were at our full potential yet so would be Bonifaz and Joseph. However Joseph was no fighter, and we had the element of surprise on our side. I approached and attacked from the front, without warning, destroying the door and ripping through the main hall in search of those two Verraters.

Kristoph had come in through the back and headed upstairs. I heard the fight, snarls, and growling, the cracking of walls and furniture, and then I followed quickly. I saw them both, Kristoph and Joseph, in wolf form, engaged in a physical battle, but it was over quickly. Kristoph had thrown him through a second-story window and out in the courtyard. It was then I felt a presence behind me, it was Bonifaz and I looked forward to this confrontation. His attack was quick and furious, but he was overmatched by my rage for revenge and I overtook him. I bit his cheek and felt my by fangs dig deeply into his flesh, it was sour. I clawed at his face while he ripped open my shoulder with a strong bite, and then retaliated by leaping at him and returning a bite to his forearm. I remember we tumbled down the staircase breaking the railing and destroying a cherry wood table. It was a fight to the death and I recall having the advantage, until the gunshots.

Outside was a mob of twenty or more men, angry and armed with muskets and swords. Their smells were unrecognizable, as were their faces. They were not of this town yet ready to defend it. I remember someone entering the estate, coming through the hallway as Bonifaz and I continued our fight. Shots were heard again and Bonifaz was struck in the face, then in the chest. He fell as I looked up seeing more people storming the house. They were shouting and screaming but the rage from denying me my revenge consumed me. I remember being quick with the feeling of hatred deep my veins. Hatred was not normal in wolf form, or any emotion for that matter, it was always more pure, instinctual, and insatiable appetite. I have experienced that with more the

Changing, I had become more conscious in the wolf form, but my emotions were never this subjective. Perhaps it was because Bonifaz's death did not satisfy me, I felt cheated, and justice was not served. I feel that now, but why did I in wolf form. Then I realized, perhaps the myth was true, Wolfened. Was my time coming?

At the estate, I remember ripping the mob part after being shot in the leg. I was only grazed so I continued to fight easily, I remember screams and shouting of vulgar gestures as I moved through bodies, ripping and clawing them apart. I saw Kristoph outside in the courtyard doing the same. Then I remember someone shouting. "It's a nest, It's a nest we must retreat." (A nest? Wolves do not construct nests... how ignorant, how crass.)

It was the last thing I recall. I woke up this morning and saw puddles of blood in hallways, so much had spilled, the furniture had been destroyed, and the walls were covered with entrails and skin. It was applauding, and the smell was foul, yet I stood in the middle of it all, detached by the grotesque scene. The act we had committed put a bright light on us all and brought everything into perspective. Our feeble quarrel over gold and packs brought only the death of innocent men and perhaps left children fatherless and women widowed. The guilt was overwhelming, and I began to pray right there again. This time aloud, I did not care who heard me. I asked for forgives and understanding, and it seems I got something in return. I had an epiphany.

Bonifaz was killed by gunshot wounds, how was this possible? I remember Dierk being shot, but it only affected him in human form. Therefore, the question, "how could one be brought down by gunfire in wolf form?" arose. I walked over to Bonifaz's body, and while inspecting the wounds I notice the bullet inside his chest. I grabbed some tongs that lay on the kitchen floor and removed it. The projectile was silver, pure silver, they had made silver weapons!

Somehow that mob knew of our existence, even more so of our weakness. This was not some random act of angry locals, we were being hunted. I wrapped the bullet up in spare cloth and placed it in my pocket. I was confused and awestruck, someone had to have done research on us, or perhaps had a confrontation with one of us before. Either way...there were hunters out there now.

MY WOLF WITHIN 1750-1783

Quickly I went to find Kristoph; he was upstairs in the hallway and had just awoken. I was relieved to find my friend all right, as he was leaning up against a closet door. Behind it, we heard whimpering and I quickly opened it only to find Joseph there, cowering in the dark. He too was bloodied with a cut on his forehead and a bruised neck. He begged for his life and I will admit I wanted to, but Kristoph stopped me and stated Joseph had saved his life.

It seems Kristoph had followed Joseph outside after he had thrown him through the window. Once the mob arrived they had ceased their fighting and joined forces, He helped Kristoph fight off the hunters and stopped one of them from shooting him in the back. I was frustrated and growled while grabbing him. I pulled him out of the battered wardrobe and could smell the fear on him along with another stench. Familiar now but not before, I knew what it was... the smell of deceit. It was he who had been behind this whole thing, the cave-in, the hunters. I shouted, "Tell me what is going on! Why were there hunters here, why do they possess silver weapons?" Joseph pleaded for his life and confessed all his knowledge on terms that we did not kill him. I dragged him downstairs, commanding him to sit on the bloodstained couch and reveal everything. He did and started to tremble, nearly sobbing, then but drew in a breath and enlighten us on this whole fiasco.

He began with the cave-in and I immediately accused him of staging that, but he swore it was not of his or Bonifaz's doing, instead just horrible luck. When it was over Bonifaz, Kristoph and he had made it out, but Kristoph was unconscious and wounded. Instead of helping him, they took the gold and returned to the estate. The next day they wanted to celebrate, but since this city was abandoned, they traveled to the next town over and planned for a night of alcohol and prostitutes. Embarking on their night of chaos, they attended a show at the theater. In their drunken shape, Joseph offered to buy the entire establishment a round of whiskey then presented the proprietor with gold ingot. Being a businessman he instantly recognized the seal, and knew at that exact point it had been stolen from the World Bank of France.

I intervened and told him no it was from the mine. Joseph thought that as well, but it seems the mine was not being used for gold, it was for coal, and Bonifaz fabricated that whole story. He, himself, had stolen it many years ago before the two had met and had hidden it in the mine, thinking it was abandoned. To his surprise, it was not and he was never able to retrieve it with all the townspeople working inside. He later figured he needed a pack to kill off everyone and that was the real reason why he would not leave this city.

I nodded as Kristoph threw his hands up in disbelief. Bonifaz was not interested in the pack or traditions; he was just a thief and a murderer who needed pawns to do his dirty work, what a fraud. The truth brought much light to our situation but I failed to see how the silver came into our midst so I told Joseph to continue. He claimed the theater owner quickly informed the constable without their knowledge and they were followed back to a tavern, it was then raided. There was a fight, and a woman struck Bonifaz with a silver crop and deeply wounded him. The entire room witnesses the events and then we Changed. We destroyed the inn and killed all those within it, a few townspeople were in the streets as we fled and watched the whole thing erupt. They must have tracked us back to the estate and planned to take the gold as well.

Joseph you idiot, you have robbed me of avenging Ms. Lauren and now doomed us all. I was awestruck by his stupidity but almost found this to be humorous. Perhaps this was the initial step into madness for me. I started to laugh and Joseph snickered in his nervous state. He was that stupid and it shocking.

I then asked him where the rest of the gold was stored and he had placed it in the basement where I was caged. I told them we needed to grab as much as we could carry, flee the estate, and split up for good. Joseph pleaded not to leave him alone and that he could not survive without a pack. I found his behavior pitiful but Kristoph told me that he would stay with him until his debt was repaid. Joseph thanked us both and promised he would never betray us again.

At that point, I did not care where his allegiance was; I just knew we needed to leave this place immediately. It was destroyed and they...them... the hunters... not only knew of our existence but our den as well. I told them both to get the gold as I walked outside in search of any way of transportation. Luckily, I found and few horses that were tied to a tree down the road, they must have been left behind by the mob. We loaded their satchels with much of the gold, filled out pockets as well, and headed out of this forsaken city. A sense of freedom filled my mind; at last, we would be rid of this place.

MY WOLF WITHIN 1750-1783

December 30th, Saturday 1780

Two years have passed since my last entry, the reason being that nothing eventful has happened. Kristoph, I, along with Joseph have traveled across Prussia in search of a suitable den but only found temporary dwellings. I did manage to locate an appropriate refuge a few weeks ago by a river, but due to a deluge, we lost our residence. While evacuating the area we became acquainted with a gentlemen of…our own kind. He was in search of his companion while crossing our territory and offered us some information if we let him pass in peace.

Our encounter was brief as he spoke of a sadistic woman whose father had been slain in a wolf conflict of some sort. He was unaware of her name but claimed she was from the northern regions, avenging her father's murder by hunting our kind. Rumors suggested she had been doing this for months and her death toll so far was 23. Four weeks before we had encountered this man, the woman had slaughtered his pack. He escaped and wished to search for his companion in peace so we allowed him on his way. Other than that, we have had no other meetings with our kind. That was a year ago today.

In recent months, we had hunted well, but winter had come faster than expected. Kristoph spoke of a man he knew that might still live in this area. His name was Ru'var Klaut, and Kristoph had known him from a previous pack. It seems there was a war of words many years ago and his old pack had disbanded. He did not go into detail, which was understandable. The experiences I have had with packs do not bear well with me either, but our kind needs a pack to survive especially if such a vindictive woman is on the rise.

A few nights ago, we took refuge in an abandoned farmhouse that we simply referred to as "The Haus" and conversed more about this Ru'var. Kristoph spoke of him highly and stated he had to lead many packs in his days and knew of other territories with good prey. I think he was requesting we find a leader without trying to offend me but I took no offense. I had survived the betrayal of two packs but I was far from leading one. I trusted Kristoph's instincts and if he believed we needed Ru'var, then we did. We all agreed to find him and headed out to the last place Kristoph figured he would reside.

We found ourselves in Holstein, Hamburg where many people were thriving. They were still relieved and boasted about the Seven Years War ending due to the Treaty of Hubertertusburg signed 17 years ago. At the present, the town itself seemed untouched by any wolfs. The people were kind to outside travelers and held a happy presence about them. They possessed innocence that I not only found refreshing but also a trait of easy prey. We posed as traders passing through, exchanging our gold for goods, and blended in quite nicely. At the local tavern, there was a woman named Rose who we had met. She was kind and a bit forward but we welcomed her company, or at least I did for the night. She satisfied my temporary needs and Joseph chuckled like a little boy while watching our public affection for each other. Kristoph warned me it was a mistake mixing with locals, but Rose had provided a warm bed and place for the three of us to take shelter in. She was very attractive and yet I sensed low self-esteem from her. (Dare I say I took advantage?) Rose had mentioned a past relationship that went amiss and left her will continuous doubt in herself. I acted interested but was only concerned about what she could provide for us. Sex for me and shelter for my companions was suitable for now. I couldn't become attached, for we would need to hunt soon then once again relocate.

The next morning we left her home without her knowledge and hunted that night. We traveled a few miles and feasted on a caravan who had departed town a few days before our arrival. They wouldn't be missed for months and that would give us enough time to find Ru'var. While the others returned to The Haus, I returned to Rose's establishment for the night. I was welcomed with more intimate favors, for she had taken a liking to me. Over the next few days, I found her dissatisfying, I knew she was a kind person, but lingering over my every move caused me to become irate very quickly. I sent her out to inquire about a Ru'var to the locals and in her absence, I secretly regrouped with my brothers. We contemplated our next move. She did return later with information from those who had heard of the name.

We decided that Rose's abode was far better than The Haus to reside in, or at least until we found Ru'var. The hunting was fair and Rose was considered our servant. Those two teased me with the courtship I had with such a naïve and needy woman. I supposed she did possess an inexperienced look on life but having no inkling as to whom or what we were made this house safe.

For the past two months, we had been living here, hunting in the night on far away prey or drunken fools who have wandered from town. Our Changing's have evolved significantly! I actually could concentrate as well as communicate with the others during the hunts. We have become an improved…situation but still lacked good leadership. While resting during the day, Rose would fetch clothes and supplies. She made a good overseer. I must admit taking advantage of this woman did not sit too well with me, but this was survival. We were on a level she could never understand. I feared she would learn the truth soon and that would surely bring her demise. I did not rather it not come to that, so I hope we find Ru'var before then. We will continue this charade until the time comes to alter the plan.

January 5th, Friday 1781

The holidays this year were very delightful. I have not felt that much joy in a long time. Rose had made an exquisite meal at Christmas and invited a few of her friends to join us that evening. They then returned on News Year Eve and entertained Joseph and Kristoph in ways only women can. The six of us had quite an eventful night without ever leaving the house. One of them, Jillian I recall, actually gave us a potential lead of Ru'var's whereabouts. It seems he had lived in the neighboring town and made his way to Holstein a few days ago. The rumor was he passed through the area looking for supplies but we knew better. He was hunting and found himself in Hamburger the next morning. If this were true, Ru'var was very clever for we did not smell or sense him at all. If he did indeed hunt, he did it downwind, which was a trick used by the experienced and resourceful. Kristoph was right, he did obtain skills, skills he could teach us.

Later that night as the women left and Rose went to bed, the three of us transpired our plans. Joseph presented that if Ru'var was hunting in this area, we could pose as prey to get his attention. I shook my head at his lack of common sense. If he were hunting, he would be in wolf form, as would we, which could prove to be difficult considering two wolf situations hunting on the same ground would not end well. (Not to mention our scent would give us away.) That is when I had the idea of setting Rose afoot on this quest. They laughed and whispered that only I would send my beloved to her impending doom. The thing is I never considered her my beloved, for I do not love Rose, I see her as only a convenience. I know that is not honorable, but I do it to save my brethren, and that should justifiable enough. Only God's judgment will decide.

They were highly amused that Rose would be the bait and now we needed a strategy. How was I going to get Rose to travel in the night...alone...without me? I hoped no harm would come to her, but if it were to happen, it would bare me the confrontation of leaving her for good. I informed them we should sleep, and regroup in the morning, by then a solution should present itself.

January 6th, Saturday 1781

This morning I awoke tired and worn, for there was no moon last night, therefore no hunt. It had been quiet, almost too quiet and this allowed my thoughts to run wild. I am still conflicted about Rose but there was simply no other way. At breakfast, the food did not satisfy us so instead, we used the time for discussion and reviewed the matter in detail. While Rose slept in, we calculated the entire event and were confident that it would fare well for all of us. If only I could get to Rose before Ru'var was to attack her then maybe, she would survive. That is if I could resist the Urge to hunt her myself.

We were to have a good portion of meat stored before the hunt and feast before the Changing. This was unorthodox for we never ate previous to a hunt, why would we? So perhaps there is a chance we might not even change, and with the moon in its last cycle, she may not be strong enough. This whole thing would be based on hypothesis so we shall see. Tonight Rose and I will be attending a play, afterward, I will arrange another date for tomorrow evening. It will be then our plan will take effect. In the meantime, I ponder my thoughts further on this matter.

January 7th, Sunday 1781

Last night our date went well and the play was very entertaining, we retired back to Rose's establishment where we became intimate. It was nice to be alone with a woman while Kristoph and Joseph were back at The Haus. I feel her emotions towards me have grown and I sense myself becoming more accustomed to her presence. Though I see no future for us, I am Wolf and in she is not...it is that simple.

I arranged another date with her this evening at the local tavern, perhaps at nightfall, we shall leave and go for a stroll through the town. It will be chilly but I intend to keep her warm by bringing an extra coat. My nerves are worn but I trust Kristoph and Joseph will be guarding my safety. If Ru'var does arrive, we shall be ready for him.

January 9th, Tuesday 1781

We have done it! We have found Ru'var! The plan did not go as intended however, it did present us with a better opportunity to speak with him. Two nights ago as Rose and I left the tavern, she agreed to accompany me on a late-night walk. She wrapped her arm around mine and braced her head against my shoulder. It felt good to feel her close to me, but I tried to dismiss my feelings and focused on the plan. We walked through the town's inner courtyard and cut across the bridge that overlapped the small stream. It was frozen solid and we stopped to witness its beauty. As we continued, I suggested we go by the park and gaze upon snow-covered pine trees. She agreed and while reaching the park's entrance, I stopped as I noticed the moon emerging from the clouds.

It was strong but not at its full potential, I still felt the Urge, but not as strong. Feasting before the night had come did restrain me. I hoped I would not change, as my senses were heightened I smelled the alcohol on Rose and concluded she was intoxicated. I laughed and realized this aided my situation. For any oddity, she would witness this night could surely be dismissed as just an overindulgence of brandy.

I felt the moon staring at me but I fought it hard and that is when I heard the howl. It was a wolf...or wolfish and Rose jumped almost straight into my arms. She asked it if were the beast the townsfolk heard about, the lore of wolf and man combined to form a horrible creature. I acted unconcerned, told her it was nonsense, and wished us to stay in the park a little longer. We heard it again and I told her to stay still as I investigated the nearby woods. She protested of course, but I needed her to be alone if Ru'var was to seek a victim. I ran into the woods as I heard Rose yell my name. I think she tried to follow but she could not keep up with my speed. I took the position behind a large tree and saw Rose now standing by herself in a clearing. Looking around and yelling for me. I must admit, her in distress did make me uncomfortable, but my urges started to see her as prey so I focused my thoughts on Ru'var. I smelled the air and sensed Kristoph close, he must be scouting there as well.

Joseph was also here but upwind...fool! Ru'var might smell him before Rose. He would retreat if he sensed another wolf is present. I sighed and waited long as I continued to hear Rose in a panic. I shouted out to her to give her reassurance, told her to stay still and I would be back soon. Her screaming halted as she heard me respond and whispered, "Where are you?"

I neglected to answer as I heard Ru'var howl again. It echoed through the cold night, he was close and I knew he would be quick. Having a full stomach did help with the Changing but Kristoph ate light so he probably had already changed. He was tracking Ru'var well, but Joseph worried me. He was not in control while in was in wolf form and could jeopardize our success.

I heard Ru'var once more and then Rose screamed as she saw something in the shadows. I ran out of the woods towards her in hope Ru'var would be alerted of my movement and I was right. He leaped out after me and pounced on my back, I was knocked to the ground, and in my fall, I was able to get a glimpse of him. Completely in wolf form, tall, with a darkish brown coat and an onyx mane, he was magnificent. A perfect specimen of our kind, vicious and unforgiving, He came at me, but I showed no fear and countered his attack. He was taken off guard, I could sense it and his smell changed. I think it was fear or confusion. I was in human form but with wolf-like strength and speed. He seemed bewildered at first, but shifted his attention away from me and lunged for Rose. I heard her shout, and as Ru'var advanced, I saw Kristoph emerge from the woods. Joseph quickly followed and they attacked him ferociously, but it seemed to be more of a territorial fight than to the death. In the excitement, I tried to control myself but then the clouds drifted apart. The moon became so bright that I felt it happening. I was losing control and I roared to Rose to run, she did thank God. I felt myself give in and change, but I have learned to manage the rage...to a point.

In wolf form, I joined my pack members as we beat Ru'var down. Joseph had bitten him lightly but drew enough blood to cause him to run off. Kristoph followed, as I did until Joseph lost his control. He circled back and went after Rose, with his speed I knew he would be on top of her in minutes.

I went after him. It was that decision that initiated matters to turn for the worst. He had corned Rose by the bridge and her screams alerted some passing villagers. There were two men, one with a pitchfork, and the other a lantern. They retaliated by swinging the light toward Joseph's eyes, in a cheap attempt to distract him from Rose. They were brave men and I was grateful, they are actions allowed me to pounce on Joseph, causing us to scuffle. He snarled but I showed my dominance and he submitted quickly. Rose, however, had run off by that time, as well as the villagers, and now aware of our presence.

Shortly after, I returned to The Haus, but this morning I saw no sign of Kristoph. I hoped our little scuffle did not alert more hunters. If so Joseph once again had blundered our opportunity and I would be dammed if I were left to lead this fool alone. Now I await our companion's arrival. I hope he returns before we are chased away from this place. I have not checked up on Rose either, perhaps it is time I tell her I am leaving soon.

January 10th, Wednesday 1781

I am relieved to write that Kristoph had returned later this afternoon and with news of Ru'var's location. He had tracked him to his den and waited until the next day to return. It was a cave far outside of town, to the south in a mountain range. This was why Kristoph had been gone for so long. In wolf form, the trip was easy, but with human feet, the terrain was very difficult. He spoke that Ru'var had been wounded, leading a blood trail to his whereabouts. Ru'var had retired there for the night but in the morning he did not emerge, which means his injuries were worse than we anticipated. If he was still in his den healing, then now was the time to seize him. We grabbed the horses and proceeded to his lair. I hoped that we would still find him before nightfall.

January 11th, Thursday 1781

Last night we reached Ru'var's den only to find him missing. His scent had faded but the blood was fresh, telling us he healed enough to move on. Hoping he was still close, we returned to town. To our surprise, many Villagers were out and had been alerted to the events of the past nights. They were angry and had formed search parties, combing every street and alley with torches. If Ru'var had fully healed, he still would not be able to flee with the mobs afoot. They were too large and he would be seen eventually. If I were he, I would be hiding in town somewhere, waiting for the people to disperse. I told Joseph to check on Rose while I waited at the Tavern. I told him if she were to ask for me, to tell her I was presently indisposed and that I will come to her soon. I know he was incompetent but this should keep him occupied while the masses were out. I hope that he would not make a mess of this.

He left then a few moments later Kristoph entered the tavern and we observed the grounds for anything unusual. We noticed more men with muskets and torches scouting out the area but no beast had been spotted. Many of them I didn't recognize but then I saw a man at the bar with a neck wound, I nodded in his direction towards Kristoph, but before he looked that way, the man turned around and glanced straight at me. He approached us and acknowledged Kristoph first, an icy grin appeared on his face.

"Kristopher Wells I presume, it's been a long time". He said and Kristoph smiled back. My anxiety lowered at that point, why not it could be this easy in the first place. It seemed they were on good terms as Ru'var invited us to sit by the fire. I sat in a chair and listened to the stories of their adventures in France many years ago. For Ru'var was Corsican, they were from a noble and strong region. He shook my hand as we were introduced and then he caught my scent and became angered. I assured him that our encounter a few nights prior was not personal and that I...we... needed to get his attention. He was not pleased that Joseph had injured him yet showed no sign of hostility towards Kristoph's attack. That night I learned certain quarrels were dismissed among wolfs in human form. The roles of strength switched between the Changing. In wolf form, one could hold Alpha status but in human form, that same individual could be reduced to Omega. It was complicated but I felt I understood. We spoke of The Haus and invited him back; he agreed, stating he was happy to get out of his depressing cave. Dodging the search parties, we reached our home quickly and then did not hesitate to discuss the matter further. We told him outright we needed him as our leader. He was undecided and stated he did not know Joseph or me very well. The trust would have to be earned and to do that we must hunt together. I of course agreed, but Joseph had not come back from Roses yet. I told them we should check on him, but he walked through the door at that very moment.

He was troubled and stated that Rose had company, a woman named Diana. He instantly felt a bad feeling from her but did not want to depart in haste, for the sake of displacing suspicion and stayed in the hope to learn more about this strange woman. Perhaps Joseph was getting smarter after all. He told us he had arrived first and reassured her that I would see her soon. Unknown to him, Rose had still been upset with me, so prior to Joseph's arrival, she had invited this Diana to come by to comfort her. Once Rose allowed her into her home, she introduced them to each other. A round of pleasantries ensued but then their conversation switched to...werewolves. This Diana asked many questions for somehow she knew of Roses encounter with us. Joseph claimed she had to be a hunter and perhaps the same woman we had heard about a few years ago.

Ru'var listened intensely and now seemed to be more eager to take control of the pack. He broke the silence and told us tomorrow we will hunt together. From there we shall see how well we function as a pack. This hunt will hold the outcome for our future. I am enthusiastic and yet terrified.

January 12th, Friday 1781

Early this morning I awoke to the voices of Ru'var and Kristoph laughing. I assume they were reminiscing throughout the night. It was good to see my friend in high spirits. (I on the other hand felt a little distraught and weak from the events of the past nights but it was well worth the discomfort.) Ru'var was an undeniably a good addition, or at least for now. He struck me as a charismatic fellow with stout and strength. His appearance was of an older man with much experience in his eyes. I am sure I have much to learn from him.

After the first encounter between him and Kristoph, I was lucky to get Rose and myself out of there safely. Oh, my...Rose I will need to see here this morning or perhaps after lunch. I might send Joseph over there again with a message. No... I know she will be upset with me so that may be a bit rude. I will go there myself after we converse on our next step of action.

January 13th, Saturday 1781

After I made my entry yesterday morning, I had spoken with the rest of the group, for there was much to address. During our assembly, Ru'var informed us he and Kristoph were members of a pack a few years ago but were split up after a massacre they had committed. It was a large hunt of about eight wolfs and over thirty victims. It was graphic but I was not shaken, for violence is becoming a tradition. It is amusing that at one time, I found myself sick and full of remorse, but now I accepted it. However, I know it still is not natural.

We are cursed and may even be spawns of Lucifer himself, but if we are truly evil, then why do I pity these humans so? Why do I pray for them and not for my own forgiveness? My faith in the almighty father is still strong, but if he has forsaken me, then so be it. If my final days I will be judged before he and only he will decide my punishment. For now, I must learn as much as possible about past hunts and prey. It will be this knowledge that will increase my chances of survival.

I projected my thoughts back to Ru'var as he told us how he prepared for such a large hunt. Joseph paid attention with wide eyes like a child listening to a bedtime story. I took mental notes, on flanking procedures, different smells for each emotion. I learned of placement, where pack mates positioned themselves when moving in on prey and mostly how to pick the ill or old for the feast.

He spoke of the settings of the moon, the cloud formations, and the changing of the wind. These were all clues on the moon's future strengths and settings for the oncoming nights. I knew the importance of the moon but not like this. Ru'var was a good teacher and I had asked a few questions myself. I inquired about how one remembers the hunts and our consciousness during the Changing. He told me it was all about the experience, the more you do, the more in tune you become. He then spoke of the dangers of hunters and that he had been shot and even impaled on one accession. "Most wolfs make the same mistake, if you stay in one area too long, you attract attention. Soon town constables start to ask questions, and then mobs would come. You must leave and find somewhere far enough to start again. It is a never-ending process." Ru'var continued his lectures, he was amazing, he had escaped death multiple times, confronted entire towns alone, and even faced off with other packs. This was all so interesting since I have only seen a few of our kind and assumed we were low in numbers. However, according to Ru'var there or many of us, we are just spread thin.

His tone suddenly switched, he became quiet, and then spoke of the New Land, far away across the sea. They had recently become victorious from some sort of revolution with England and were now establishing their independence. Many people were sailing there and he had hoped to reach the "Promised Land" by attempting to find an affordable ship. It was all so inspirational, and I found Kristoph to be equally excited. He asked me if I would like to travel there someday. I thought it was most unlikely, but the idea did sound captivating.

Later we decided to prepare for the coming night. Tonight's moon would be full, making us a force to be reckoned with. Hunters were about, so we needed to be careful and required a sensible plan. We concluded to meet at Ru'var's old den in the woods at sunset. We would all leave The Haus one by one, not to raise suspicion, and on our way out of town observe the search parties who were still present.

I told them I had a prior engagement and that I would meet them there at the first hint of night. I thanked Ru'var and headed off to Rose's by taking one of the horses from the stable. I rode fast knowing I would not have a lot of time. I was contemplating how to make this woman mad enough to dismiss my presence early, but not so much that she would never want to see me again.

While I reached her home, I walked up to the porch and gently knocked. I held a bouquet of tulips I had picked on the way from some poor scheibkerl's garden. I knocked again as I heard voices and then the door opened. Rose looked at me and I smiled, as I was delighted to see her, she was not amused. Quietly she walked out on the porch and asked me in a whisper what I wanted. I told her I was here to apologize and she just stared at me.

She was not quite herself and I understood, seeing werewolves was a frightful sight, and leaving her behind might just be unforgivable. I apologized again and told her that I searched for her all night and how relieved I was that she was unharmed.

Rose believed my sincerity because she hugged me and claimed she was so frightened that she could never leave her home during the night again. I held her but noticed shadows in the windows. I asked if she had company and she nodded then brought me into the house. A woman sat on the couch, a man accompanied her. He was standing behind her as a butler might. Rose introduced her as Diana and the man was Dean, both were from Britain and researching content for her new novel. Something was off with this woman and then I remember Joseph had spoken of a Diana. If this was the same one, I understand why he felt uneasy around her. She seemed to be analyzing me, searching for something, a weakness, or any odd behavior on my part. Perhaps it was for her book and when I asked her about its subject matter, she stated it was regarding "Unique Wildlife", interesting indeed.

I stayed only for a few more minutes then left Rose on good terms. She had forgiven me, but I assumed it would be a very long time before we would engage in a sexual activity soon. She was scared to death, and this Diana must now be staying with her, comforting her. Was she a relative, and friend, who was she, and where did she come from? I would soon find out, but it was getting dark and time to meet back at Ru'var's Den.

I rode the horse until the terrain got too rough, and then walked the rest of the way. I saw my pack and they greeted me with open arms. It was good to feel a part of something, even Joseph seemed to be in good spirits no longer the little wurm as I remember him. I asked what our target was and Ru'var stated that after I left for Roses they obtained information on another caravan entering the town. It would pass through these woods in about 30 minutes and by them, we could feast in quiet. After that, split up and meet in the morning at The Haus.

We agreed and the events that followed were of wonderment and awe. I remember the Changing, the smells again, and the Urge for blood. The moon, she was so bright and I completely gave myself to her power. I moved with grace and struck with such a procession. The caravan was exactly where Ru'var had said it would be with three wagons and two horses. Two men were leading with guns but never fire off a shot. For Joseph and Kristoph had taken them within seconds. I approached the side and flanked them as Ru'var came from the rear. The horses panicked and tried to turn around, but they were struck down as well. I heard screams and the scent of fear filled my snout. It was wonderful, the taste, the smell, and the full stomach, it seemed to last all night and I wanted it too, but in real-time it was only a few minutes. We broke off when we saw torches coming and realized a nearby search party must have heard the screams. Alerted, I heard them shout a call as they were approaching, but their attempt for a rescue was in vain. We had slaughtered the entire caravan, feasted well, and fled before any of them saw anything. I ran to the north and saw my brothers split to the south and east. Ru'var went with Joseph, and I planned to circle back in the morning and make it home just before sunrise, which I did.

When I arrived, I found Kristoph on the porch alone. He was standing, facing the dirt road, eyeing something. I glanced where he was looking and saw her, Diana. She was wearing a green shawl over her shoulders, a matching hat, and speaking to the woman who lived in the house across the way. As she left the woman's porch Kristoph turned and scolded me with a harsh tone. "I told you not to get out of your bed this morning, your too sick to roam around now get back in the house." I knew what he was doing and I limped inside making quick eye contact with the woman. She gave me a frown, no matter; I returned it with a crooked smile.

As Kristoph followed me inside, he closed the door behind us and asked if I saw Joseph or Ru'var yet. I said no and he just nodded. He knew they were resourceful and would return but his face still held a troubled look. He said we had to leave this town immediately and when I asked him why he stated that he saw Diana last night. He had circled the mob returning home and claimed he saw her with them. I asked him if he was sure of what he had seen. He countered my questioning by stating it was dark, but he recognized her scent. He smelled her in wolf form and there was no mistake. That was it then, Diana was indeed the hunter we had predicted and would need to speak with Ru'var most urgently.

January 15th, Wednesday 1783

Two days had passed since my last entry and although things seem to be quiet at the moment, much conspiring has taken place. The four of us have been debating over the issue of this Diana dilemma. Joseph suggested we deal with her face to face, but Ru'var insisted we find out more about this woman first, who she is, and where she had come from. I agreed and would ask Rose more questions once she and I rekindled our relationship.

The past nights I had been to her home and found out that she and Diana were once roommates at the University of Konigsberg a few years ago. They had become good friends and then separated after graduation only to reconnect recently. Their story was bland, but we knew there was more going on. Diana was with the search parties, asking questions, observing us. Redefining a friendship was a deception, one Rose could not see past. Spending so much time with Rose only meant she was onto us or at least had a hunch of our existence. I figured we kept our secret well, but we were still a new pack and unorganized. However, the element of disbelief and dismissal of our past was always in our favor and kept us unseen. Werewolves simply do not exist and for those who find out the truth do not live long to speak of it. Ru'var insisted that Kristoph search the university records and deeds, find the history of this town. Perhaps this Diana owned property, if so we may find her surname. I informed I would see Rose again this afternoon and would inquire about the woman some more. They agreed and then we moved onto more pressing matters,

The search parties were growing and questions for the missing had been raised. Every night it was getting harder and harder to be inconspicuous. The town's people had been alerted to something odd happening within the streets and their panic spread. I notice more constables were now patrolling in groups of two. Luckily, no incidents have occurred in the last three days and the moon would not be full for another four. I trust this these events will end soon and then we could flee this place. Joseph had been the one who found The Haus, he had an eye for such things. I may ask them if it would be a wise decision to send him out alone in search of a new den. It would have to be far away with plenty of prey. Kristoph or I could go with him but that would split up the pack and with a potential threat in the vicinity, it may prove to be an unwise move. I shall think about this later but for now, I head for Roses home.

January 16th, Thursday 1783

Last night I courted Rose to the courtyard. It was the first time she had been out of her house since the unpleasant incident. With the quietness of the pack and constables patrolling, I think she began to feel safe again. It was a cold night and she hugged my arm and shoulders as we strolled through the cobblestone path. It led to the frozen pond in her backyard and she enjoyed watching a light mist of snow blow across its icy surface. She smiled in delight and it was good to see Rose become her old self again.

After our stroll, we returned to the house and enjoyed hot coffee as I read a passage from Broom Hilda to her. She smiled as I joked about such a story then we started to share our experiences of school. I told her I was premedical and had to leave the school do to my mother's illness before she passed away. It was a half-truth, but that happened many years ago and she would never find the real reason I left.

I picked the topic of school hoping she would bring up her dorm room or friends, she did, but none of Diana. I figured I needed to pry a bit deeper and openly asked about roommates, but she seemed to be avoiding the subject…that was until I got bold. "Tell me about your friend Diana," I insisted and felt the room got cold, I smelled her growing uncomfortable and then her fear, but why was she afraid? I asked her who the woman was, but only received the same information as before, she was a roommate that was all. No last name, no story on how they met, I received nothing new. She was hiding the details well, and I told her she was too vague about someone who she considered to be a close friend. Rose pushed away even harder with only silence. I was not getting anything from her, so perhaps Kristoph would find more on this Diana. Then the conversation altered with Rose beginning to interrogate me. She said Diana told her I would be asking her many questions, and asking such questions was rude. I was in confusion, had this Diana predicted my coming here? If so, she must have told Rose she was a hunter and that we were...no that was impossible, I was being paranoid. I demanded Rose tell me how much Diana new about me, my friends, The Haus, and Rose became very uncomfortable then stood up to face the fireplace. She stared into its flames and became very quiet. I asked her once more and she stated that was something going on between Diana and myself, something odd and she did not want to be in the middle of it anymore. She then became loud and displeased, telling me that if we had any more questions we should be asking each other. I sensed she was pressured and perhaps I added to this mess. I tried to shift the conversation back to a light-hearted tone by stating it was a wonderful idea and we should meet. We should get to know each other, I fed her a lie that she was my one true love, my "Schones Madchen" and to become a bigger part of her life, I should get to know her friends. Therefore, in a moment of insanity, I suggested we hold a party, a small get together, where we would be the hosts. Rose did indeed think I had lost my mind and asked why the party should take place here. I told her since Diana and I were both friends of hers, a neutral place would be more comfortable. Besides, the fact that my establishment was that of bachelors, it just was not suitable for women. Rose at first was uncertain but then warmed up to the idea. I told her that an evening with friends and merriment would lighten the mood of the town. She agreed and we started to make preparations. The party would be two nights from now, a perfect setting. The moon would not be out and that would perhaps give us a good disguise. If Diana were to show up, a face-to-face confrontation would bring a lot to the surface. We would then know her true intentions, and if lucky, perhaps her weaknesses.

January 17th, Friday 1783

I had spoken with the pack first thing this morning and informed them of my party idea, Ru'var found it careless, and I was chastised for it. I did convince the others to join me but Ru'var reminded us that in the past, hunters had been successful in thinning our existence. He warned never to underestimate them. A veteran wolf killer would be too much of a match for me, and if Diana was an experienced hunter she would have a team, they always had a team I was told, "Expect to be outnumbered." Joseph tried to defuse the situation by claiming there would not be a moon that night so we should not be concerned. I reminded them the party was a mere rouse, and mu sole purpose was to obtain more information and not indulge in the festivities. "There will be guests, guests do to drink, and secrets are fairly spilled in the presence of alcohol". They agreed to attend, but only if Ru'var constructed a secondary plan in the case of an emergency. I told him we would have one but not until Kristoph told us what he had found.

When Kristoph did return, we gathered around a small table and he presented us with a few documents sealed with a wax emblem. It was the seal of the University of Konigsberg and I knew what these papers contained. Diana did indeed attend school in Prussia and her transcripts proved it, but these were for a psychology major. However, during her second year, she had switched her studies to wildlife behavior and zoology. We found this odd but Kristoph continued confirming from her confidential files that her parents were mysteriously killed and their bodies discovered in a farmhouse. They lived in Hamburg in the orchard and when she had returned from holiday break, she found their mutilated bodies. The reports stated that a wild dog-like wolf had killed her family but no evidence was ever found and the case is still unsolved.

This was most interesting; she was a survivor of a hunt, and now seeks revenge. She had been doing it for years. At that moment the room filled with questions, how many of our brethren were killed by this woman? How experienced was she? How much did she know about us? Joseph started to worry and begged us to leave that instant, but Ru'var had a realization. If she were hunting our pack, she would want to flush us out, expose us to the people. She would need a night when the moon was full and wait until we changed and then set a trap. That was the reason why she joined the search party that night Kristoph had spotted her. She was not searching for victims she was hoping to see us, observe us.

It was a remarkable chain of events, if we were to leave now it would be suicide. She and her hunters were watching us and perhaps even had a trap in place already. I was convinced we should still attend the party but go on the offensive, ask questions, find answers, and then confront this Diana face to face. Our unorthodox behavior may confuse her and give us the upper hand. Tomorrow I shall see Rose again for the final preparation of the party. I will plant certain items in the house in case something were to happen until then we shall sit tight and wait for our meeting with Diana.

January 18th, Saturday 1783

Today I feel as if a storm is coming. I had never met a hunter before in fact until a few days ago I was not even sure they existed. I have been at Rose's all afternoon decorating and preparing for the party then returned to The Haus to change my attire. I will admit, I am nervous about getting ready for any kind of confrontation. Ru'var was out with Joseph training him on hunting techniques while Kristoph was looking for last-minute information, anything we could use to our advantage. As for me, I am trying to remain calm at this time and convincing myself that there is no point in fearing Diana. Nevertheless, I decided not to participate in any consumption of alcohol this evening. I need to be focused on any opposition. We shall see what the night brings.

January 19th, Sunday 1783

Last night was very interesting, to say the least, and I feel it was a catalyst to either a new beginning or our demise. We attended the party at Roses as planned, Ru'var, Kristoph, Joseph, and I held ourselves in high respect. We made sure we had dressed well for the occasion and remained quiet about past events. I felt like I was with Napes again...Napes I wonder whatever became of that fool.

The sun was setting and night began to fall as we approached Rose's manor. Many constables were out patrolling and a few had bid us a good night.

Everyone in town was aware of the party and those not attending were close by. Word of her gathering spread well, after all that was our intention.

When we approached her porch, she answered before I could knock. Rose, wearing a long red gown, greeted us with a smile. However, her scent gave away her nervousness. As we entered, she had a servant take our coats and accompanied us into the family room. Drinks were available and a quartet performed Albrechtsberger's Mass in D major. It was charming and the music seemed to calm my nerves. Some of her visitors were already present and I was introduced to the local doctor and his wife, a shop owner, and one of the professors from her university. Moments later the four of us split up and mingled with the other guests. As more people arrived, I hoped Diana would attend but I did not want to ask any more questions. I played the role of Rose's male friend and use humor to set the tone. I saw Ru'var was no stranger either to social events and blended in well as Kristoph talked to a local constable outside, trying to draw out any information about the murders. (Alternatively, should I say our caravan hunt?) He even volunteered his services for the search party and I found that to be hilarious.

Joseph was speaking to a couple of young women, students no doubt, as I continued my conversation with the doctor. I asked him about the recent developments in medicine and he informed me that the field had undergone some interesting changes. Breakthroughs on human teeth, the publication of *Traite des nerfs et de leurs maladies,* and Samuel Thomas von Sommerring's study of cranial nerves. I was highly intrigued and found myself yearning to return to my studies. Oh, I wished for a lab of my own, but that seemed impossible now. I know the rest of the crowd took medicine as a bore, but I still planned to find a cure for this affliction. For one day, I might have a normal life, receive my Ph.D., settle down, and have a family. I dismissed that thought and reminded myself that was only a fantasy…for now

Time seemed to move fast and soon a few guests had departed already. I gave Ru'var a look of uncertainty about Diana, he understood and just took it in stride. Then another knock was heard and I saw Rose quickly go to the door. She opened it, Diana was standing there, and Ru'var was right, Hunters do move in numbers. She had traveled with an entourage, four dodgy-looking gentlemen, and a woman. I looked at the clock above the fireplace, it read 9:17 p.m. Strange how quickly Rose went for the door as if she were expecting them at exactly 9:17, interesting, that was usually the time when the moon was full and the Changing started. However, since no moon was out tonight we need not worry about anyone feeling the Urge.

I wasted no time and approached Diana first, taking her hand, the smell of deceit was all over her, but no fear, so perhaps she knew of the moon as well. As I spoke to her, I attempted to use my charm and pry information but all I got was the same small talk. I then excused myself and attended to the other guests as Ru'var moved in. He introduced himself with such charisma. I noticed he had Diana smiling and figured what I could not get from the woman he surely could.

I returned to Joseph and he informed that three of the men Diana had come with had left for the evening. I told him to relay that information to Ru'var and in doing so he was instructed to track them, and then return in one hour. I believe Ru'var's exact words were "Take heed and if you're discovered do not return."

Kristoph approached us at that minute and stated the constables were still baffled about the caravan murders but had a recent breakthrough. They had no leads until Diana had given them some additional information. She claimed a pack of wild wolfs were loose in the area, thus being the reason why they started the search parties. With Diana's background and expertise in bizarre wildlife, it would have been easy to manipulate the constable, especially with word of the victims being torn apart and pressure from the locals wanting answers. Kristoph had taken an oath to the constable not to repeat what news he was told but broke in within minutes by telling me...once again...hilarious.

The party was toning down and soon I found myself in the company of only Ru'var, Kristoph, Diana, and her colleagues. Everyone else had retired. I sense Rose being uncomfortable while Diana stared at us with eyes like daggers. Her smell suddenly changed, it was of hatred, but not towards me directly...it was towards... Ru'var. She addressed him as she stood from her chair. I saw one of her men checked the window as the woman moved and positioned herself by the front door. I felt they were anxious but yet confident. Their scents changed with their blood pressure rising, I sensed adrenaline and was not the only one. Ru'var stood in the center of the room and nodded to me, as he did to Kristoph. I felt a confrontation was about to happen. It was too soon, we did not have enough information. Why would Diana make her stand now? Without the moon, we could not change and if she were going to kill us, she would be murdering four innocent men in cold blood. (At least that is what it would look like to the rest of the world.)

It was then I had a horrific realization. We were not dealing with normal people we were facing Hunters. People seeking revenge, they did not care about the law or local constables and search parties. They had planned to kill us from the beginning in wolf form or not…or not. What I thought would be our advantage was our weakness. We could not change tonight, we could not become wolfs, we did not have our strength or speed. We tried to hide behind the law but instead sacrificed ourselves. How could I have been such a fool? She must have figured us out long ago and this was the trap she had sprung, but how could she have been so sure of us...Rose, Rose had betrayed me and made sure everyone left the party early for Diana to pounce.

After my recognition, there was no need to hide anymore. I told Diana that if she was planning to do anything to get it over with. The self-righteous bitch snickered at me and stated that she intended to kill all of us, but Ru'var was her main target. It seemed she had been tracking him for years, hoping to prove her assumptions were correct. That he was indeed a wolf and he was the one who had killed her parents. We had been caught up in a plot of personal revenge and now we were all going to pay for it. I looked at Rose. She stared at me with tears in her eyes, but also hatred. She called me a beast and I asked how she knew. She shouted that Diana showed her some sort of proof and that it was all she needed to accept that I was indeed a wolf. I was confused, but this was directly after the fact that Diana had shown up on her doorstep and warmed her about me a few days prior. We were victims of a conspiracy. Rose had known about me for some time now, she just needed the proof and when I offered to throw the party, Diana took that as the opportunity to kill me…us.

One of the men drew a firearm from his coat, as did Diana and then the woman. I stood ready by removing a knife I had planted the night before behind a desk, but Ru'var stopped me. He avowed that he was the one Diana wanted and pleaded for her to let us go, but she would not agree. "All wolfs must die" she shouted and pointed the barrel at him. I figured that was it and I was going to watch my friend, my leader die, but then a harsh knock was at the door. As Rose tried to answer it, the door flew open and the local constable accompanied by many men stormed the house. They had been followed Joseph and he shouted "There sir! That's the one I told you about, she plains to rob us and kill everyone." The constables then drew his weapon and pronounced Diana and her colleagues were under arrest. Joseph had come through most strangely, but I was awed by his timing and creativity. He must have waited outside instead of following the other three men, thank goodness he did.

As the constables ordered Diana to lower her weapon, Ru'var told her to do the same. 'It's over" He stated and he was right, after all, they would not believe her story, no not the truth. I saw the abhorrence in her eyes as she lowered her gun. The constable then arrested her and took into custody. I dropped the knife then stared at Rose as she started to weep. The party was declared to be over and we were instructed to go home by the authorities. I quietly told the constable Rose was taken aback by the whole incident and I would stay with her for the night. I gave him my word that I would return in the morning, he agreed but still seemed untrustworthy of me.

Before all disembark from Roses estate, I whispered to Kristoph my plan. I told him I would stay here and keep an eye on Rose, if I left her alone she might try to get Diana freed somehow. He understood and returned to The Haus with the rest of the pack, but not before turning to me with a raised brow. "Joseph," he said and shook his head. "Who would have thought?" I jested and went upstairs. I found Rose on her bed weeping but then she began screaming at me. She was afraid that I was going to kill her. I told her to be quiet and that if she remained that way, no harm would come to her. I could smell that fear on her, it was overpowering as she continued to shout. I tried to repress my anger but it slipped through and I struck her in the face. She fell onto the bed and screamed again. I warned her to be quiet but she became hysterical; she looked at me with horrified eyes, the eyes of someone looking at a monster. I hated that look for I cared for her, but all she saw me as was a wolf, a demon, something that needed to be vanquished.

I asked why she did not come to me first, why she automatically sided with Diana. She declared Diana had more proof, and that my mysterious disappearance that night at the pond was all she needed. I abandoned her in her hour of need and Diana did not. She had come to her later that night and explained what I was and what she had witnessed that night was real and not a drunken fabrication. As I fled, Diana had followed me and as I slept, she had brought Rose to watch me change back the next day. She had witnessed the Changing. This was the proof she had told me, Diana gave her.

Rose had known all this time and no matter what I said next would not solve this dilemma, so I admitted what was, and how I became the beast. I pronounced I still cared for her, but she told me no beast so vicious could love anything and that she would testify on Diana's behalf. She would tell the court it was a misunderstanding and we were the ones that tried to kill her, Diana was merely defending the place. The authorities would believe Rose. She was respected in his town, as was her family name. Tomorrow she would go to them, and then they would come after me. Again, she told me to leave and if I did not she would scream until someone came. She ran to the window and in a fit of rage…I did the unthinkable. I attacked her in my anger and hit so hard she flew over the bed. She was dazed but still tried to scream, that noise she made was so disturbing, a gurgle, whimpering came from her deformed face. The strength of my fist had broken her jaw and shattered her cheekbones. Muffled screams came from her but she was unable to open her mouth and just rolled on the floor. I remember her green eyes, they were wide and full of terror, and her smell was of ripe blood and pain…I was overtaken. It seemed even in my human form the wolf within still raged. I felt my strength grow and the animal instincts kicked in. I took her as if a predator would a wounded animal and tossed her onto the bed. My hands were around her throat, more muffles cries came from her. It was if I was outside myself watching someone else take over my body. Then I heard the twisting of bones followed by a loud snap. I say the light faded from her eyes rather quickly and her hands released their grips around my wrists. Rose was gone, what had I done? I had committed murder. I had killed the one thing I truly loved for a long time. I remember still holding her throat moments after she had passed, I could not let her go, yet I took her away.

I climbed off her limp corpse and sat on the edge of the bed in shock, my hands shaking and I started to pray for forgiveness, but I knew I had reached a point of no return. I tried to rationalize my actions telling myself I did it for my pack; I have killed this time, not for food, but protection. The emotional pain was intense and I was filled with loss. I have never felt this way before and tried to center myself but my grief was overpowering. It was the first time I felt a loss of control and started to get dizzy. I needed to focus on something; I recalled the events earlier of this night. Ru'var, Kristoph, and the conversation I had with the doctor, then Diana…Diana. I focused on her, her scent, that smug look, her plan to kill us all. How she turned Rose against me and enviably made all of this happened. Diana had been arrested and they will want to question Rose tomorrow… she will not' be here.

Things had gotten out of control but there was a solution and it was simple, no one except the pack was to survive tonight. I had to kill Diane before the sun came up. I heard a noise come from downstairs; Ru'var had returned to check up on me. I told him what had happened, his first reaction was to curse me by realized what needed to be done and agreed to help me. We wrapped her body in a rug then placed her in the cellar, the cold would preserve her corpse for a while and retain the foul smell.

I found it very difficult to concentrate on the manner, Rose was gone, yet her face still haunted me. Therefore, I turned my focus to Ru'var and warned him that if Diana were to speak to the court tomorrow they would want to question Rose. Since I was the last person to be seen with her, the constable would surely look for me, so we had to take them both out before sunrise. We needed to kill Diana but if she were locked in a cell, it would be hard to get to her.

He was convinced that the two of us could do it, but only if I stayed focused, and I assure him I would. We headed quietly into the night and to the station at the end of town. It was late and most of the constables had retired. I suspected there could be some still guarding Diana; they would have to be killed as well. We moved within the shadows and soon reached the Confinement.

Our plan though was immediately ceased when we saw that people surrounded the entire building. They carried torches and swords and some were on horseback. We hid across the road and behind some frozen hedges. My hearing was so keen I picked up what they were shouting. It seemed Diana had escaped with her men a few moments ago and now a manhunt for her group was underway. The streets would soon be filled with people and they would be going house to house. Once they reached Rose's establishment it would be certain doom for us. I told Ru'var we needed to return to The Haus and flee this town permanently. He agreed, as we headed back home I could not help wondering that Diana would return to Roses estate to see if she was all right. If she would find the body, her bloodlust for us would increase. This woman was the devil herself, always one-step ahead of us somehow.

We reached The Haus, I woke up Kristoph and Joseph I told them of Rose and Diana, the entire story, and we immediately began to pack our supplies. We fled quietly but upon traveling on the road that led out of town, we were confronted. Diana and her group, of about seven people, were facing us with their guns drawn. (She had left town but stayed within its borders, waiting for us to leave as well. It was a genius move.)

Things become hazy after that. I remember shots fired and moving quickly as my instincts took over; we were in the weaker form, but still formidable foes to our enemies. I saw Ru'var take down two men with his fists and Joseph pounce on another. Kristoph I lost sight of as I retaliated. I truly thought this was the end of us all and in a way, I welcomed it, but at the same time, I would not give in easily to the woman who made me kill my beloved Rose.

After I broke the other female's arm, I looked for Diana through the chaos of battle. More gunshots rang out and that is when I saw Joseph confiscate a musket and return fire. I think Kristoph had one as well because I recall two men with bullet holes in her chest and faces. I continued my search for Diana and then saw her among the black powder smoke. I ran towards her as she lifted her pistol and took aim. If she pulled that trigger it would be my demise, I tried to get to her before then, but I failed, I saw the smoke and felt the ball zipped past my cheek. It tore the skin and blood poured down my chin, but from her lack of skill, she missed my vital organs. Moreover, as the cloud of smoke filled my eyes, I was upon her in seconds. I pounced and she screamed but it was not that of panic or fear like Rose, it was of anger and hate, I could smell it, hatred, years of anger and rage, she unleashed it all on me, and her strength for a female was impressive. I felt kicks to my midsection and felt her nails rip the flesh on my neck. I wrapped my hand around her throat but it was no easy task, she had countered almost all of my advancements, indeed trained in hand-to-hand combat. I managed to take hold of her coat sleeve and pull her towards me, we slipped on the ice and rolled to the cold ground. I felt the snow against my bare flesh, it burned like hot coals as I fought.

I wanted to end this foul woman's life, I too wanted revenge, but I as I gazed into her eyes, I saw she wasn't that much different than myself. She had been a victim of this curse just as I was, but unlike me, she was on the other side of our equal hate for wolf kind. Her life existed for extinguishing our species while mine, temporarily, existed for its preservation. As I finally pinned her down, my fingers spread around her throat and I squeezed.

Kristoph cried out and I turned my head towards him only to see Ru'var lying on the ground. Her bullet that grazed my cheek had struck him in the head, right between his eyes. She had done that deliberately, the shot was not for me but Ru'var. I felt that loss once again, the pain, it overcame me. I clutched her throat as she choked, gagging as she kicked and punched. I saw the life in her eyes dwindle but I concluded that killing was not the answer. It would not do Rose justice and letting her die with the knowledge that she had successfully struck Ru'var was a pleasure I wished to deny her. I wished her to suffer, for that to occur, I needed to do the unthinkable. I ripped open her collar and bit her in the shoulder. My teeth sank into her warm soft flesh and torn muscle from bone. She tasted sweet and the fear was unparalleled. She screamed as I scratched her neck with my long nail, then I let her go.

Terrified, Diana staggered to her feet and winced in pain, while she grabbed shoulder. A stare of confusion and shock filled her gaze as blood ran down her dark coat and dress. She just stared at me for a few moments in silence. There are no words for her expression…fear, then pain, and then …something else. I had never that expression seen before. Perhaps it was distress.

I stood up and ran to Ru'var, but it was too late, Diana's silver ball had taken him. Kristoph came to his aid as well but looked at me in horror realizing our Alpha had fallen. He howled in anger, it was peculiar but an urge came over me to do the same, and then Joseph followed in kind. Our mournful gathering was interrupted as I heard Diana scream out obscenities. She stood there bleeding, still carrying her shoulder, and walked to us enraged. I arose to meet her advance and shouted, "This ends tonight, you have allowed for the death of an innocent, Rose deserved better, your punishment is to now live out your life as something you despise." She screamed, her voice raspy and infuriated, her eyes, mad with rage. She accused me of being delusional and it was I who had killed Rose, not her. I justified my reasoning by stating that Rose was dragged into her web of revenge and I only defended the pack and myself. His response was cold, chilling, and vowed "To kill me in time." She then jumped on the back of a passing horse and rode off.

The constable, locals, villagers, and every man for miles were now coming. They must have heard the gunshots and screams. I tried to get Kristoph to move but he stayed by Ru'var and Joseph was not leaving either. I pleaded for them to go but they refused to leave our fallen brother. The mobs had come closer and soon surrounded us, I held up my hands and honestly, I did not care if the shot me or not, they did not.

The constable dressed my wounds and later I testified that after Diana had escaped, she had returned to Rose's manor, attacked us, and killed Rose in the process. I ran home in a panic and she followed me to this spot where we decided to make our stand. During the fight, she had shot Ru'var and then fled into the woods. I believe I say something among the likes of… "She is a very disturbed woman and had disillusions of monsters…wolfs or something. If you hurry you might catch her".

The head constable shortly arrived and chose to stay behind as the search party fled into the night after her. He took Kristoph's testimony and attempted to speak with Joseph but he was too upset to declare anything so we were told to retire for the night. In the morning we would be visited by the local law authorities to make a final statement. We returned to The Haus and that is when I observed Kristoph, he is broken I fear, and sits on the couch in silence, staring at the floor as I write this. Joseph has fallen asleep by the fire and in my exhausted and wounded state, I feel I must retire as well. I shall end my entry with this... Rest in peace dear Ru'var. You shall be greatly missed.

February 1st, Saturday 1783

We buried our dearest friend in the local cemetery last week. The service was small but he was honored well. Ru'var was buried across from the plot where I also laid Rose to rest, (secretly along with my share of the gold.) Her service had been larger and I was met by her friends and relatives. They had believed my story of Diana and came to me with open arms. I was praised for trying to protect her and being wounded while fighting off a deranged woman put me in their good standing. I could not help but feel some sort of remorse, lying to her entire family, and to the entire town was not like me. I was changing and it was not for the better.

My pack attended the service with me, also receiving praise, but it was a farce. The three of us, looking like heroes when we were most certainly the villains. It is strange how when you are evil everything seems to fall into place. However, I know God has witnessed my actions, and I know I will one-day pay for them dearly, but not today.

Yesterday I spoke with Kristoph and Joseph and we all agreed it was time to leave Hamburg. However, there does not seem to be a promising place on the map. West was nothing but mountains and few outposts, to the North was the Sea. We come from the East and in the past few weeks, more and more stories of wild wolves were spreading through the area. People were now speaking openly of such things and I even heard rumors of a bounty. "A high price for those rabid wolfs hides."

We did hunt twice in the past week but the food was scarce, the winter was harsh, and finding stragglers was getting more and more difficult. We had traveled from town to town, taking what we could to survive. We were also growing sloppy without Ru'var's guidance and were almost killed on the last hunt. I know we had been seen, for a child had witnessed us slay his family. In the chaos, we were chased off by a mob but I have foreseen that child becoming another Diana…Diana, where she was? What had become of her? The feeling that we would meet again filled me and hoped I did not make the wrong decision by letting her remain alive.

That woman had much fury and making her a wolf…I fear I may have created something worse. I just want her to suffer, for Ru'var …for Rose. We will meet again and when we do, mercy shall not be granted.

February 9th, Sunday 1783

The past week has been quiet, Kristoph has not spoken of Ru'var since the funeral, and I sense something in him has changed. Losing a father figure is always difficult but I fear he may never fully recover. As if I should speak of such things, Rose has haunted my mind incessantly and last night while we hunted, I felt empty. There was no longer a bond between our pack, or should I rephrase that… our situation now. It is true, we were not a pack anymore, only broken and distant. We have not even discussed finding a new leader.

There is though some good news. We have discovered another haven inside the town of Kiel and from there we could acquire a ship. Relocating further away would be good if we can occupy it safely, somewhere new, with plenty of prey and no mobs, search parties, or hunters. I have enough of these Prussia winters, and long nights. Even the wolf in me cries for new beginnings, a place to run, new scents and smells to encounter. It sounds good and I hope this new beginning will present itself soon.

September 30th, Tuesday 1783

More months have passed and I report things have been most uneventful until this morning. I have not seen Kristoph this high spirited since before Ru'var had passed; He seems to be slowly returning to his old self again. I must say it is refreshing to see my friend excited about something for once. Hell, we are all excited. This morning he had left early without a word of where he had gone, later he returned in the afternoon, with an intriguing smirk. He called for Joseph and me to come into the dining room and as we sat around the table, he addresses us most happily. He had found a place for us to relocate. I was fascinated but I knew my friend well, his voice and mannerisms told me there was more to his story than he expressed. Joseph was too ecstatic and did not catch his body language as I did. Instead, he hung on his every word with the enthusiasm of a child, until Kristoph revealed the place he intended for us to go.

First, he reminded us of Ru'var, how he spoke about a promised land far away, where they had a revolution that freed them from England. I remembered it clearly and knew it was a dream of Ru'var to go there. Well, Kristoph had met a man with a ship that was planning to disembark tonight for this "far away land." He had made a deal with a man by the name of Captain Chrisman, that if he were to wait until tomorrow morning, we would pay him a hefty sum for passage aboard his vessel.

I did not care for this arrangement, but it seemed we had much gold left over so it was not that bad of a loss. Joseph was so cheery he nearly wet himself and all I could do was shake my head. I knew Kristoph was intelligent, but in his state of grief, I fear he may have made a grave mistake. He had already given the Captain a down payment and I sensed he was bamboozled. I figured that when we reached the docks tomorrow, we would find no ship waiting for us. I did not want to bring his spirits down so I lightly addressed a few concerns of mine, as too how where we are supposed to hunt at sea?

The trip would take months, and if we feasted on the crew how would we sail, we were not sailors. He assured me he had thought about that and advised a plan in advance. Chrisman was the Captain of the ship "The Feuervogel". A trading ship had traveled across the oceans many times and followed a route taken by most dishonest merchants. During trips, merchants would anchor their ships and trade illegally with each other to avoid taxes and other unprofitable laws. With a good chance of encountering many other ships on the way, we could set a trap for forthcoming mercantile. It was a good proposal but very precarious, we may not encounter another ship for weeks, but Kristoph seemed to have an answer to that question as well. The captain had a registry, it contained a list of ships that were traveling along that route, and if we could steal it, we could plan our attacks accordingly. It was a brilliant plan. The thought was captivating and I agreed to it wholeheartedly, but we had to leave in the morning so time was of most importance. I ran to my room and began packing that very moment, afterward I wrote this entry. I maybe not have time to write tomorrow but I shall document my further adventures soon.

October 1st, Wednesday 1783

We awoke early this morning and grabbed the supplies we had packed the night before. We left our dwelling with horses that had already been prepared for travel. (With it still being dark, our ride out of town would go unnoticed.) As we left The Haus and stepped out on the front yard, I drew in a deep breath. My lungs filled up with the cold and crisp air and I noticed the sky contained those same stars, but what would they look like on the other side of the world?

Kristoph came from the porch and asked if we were ready. I paused and closed my eyes, taking one last deep breath. I am not fond of the memories I had of this place, but I was leaving Prussia, the motherland for the first time and I realized I shall indeed miss her.

I had heard only vague things of this new world but it was all positive; A wave of new beginnings and opportunity, exactly what we craved. I envisioned reaching the shores of the new world. The possibilities would be endless, so much undiscovered land. We could rule our territory. I exhaled, said "Ready", and grabbed my sack full of clothes, smoked meats, and the two remaining bars of gold I owned. (Not counting what I left in the cemetery with Rose.) Whatever loose currency was left in my pocket would have to do for any local purchases, and I followed my brethren to the horses.

Five stallions stood in waiting, one for our supplies and the others to ride. The sun was rising but the morning wind was very cold. I buttoned my coat, climbed atop my horse, and quietly we rode out of town. We were ahead of schedule so we took a longer way, which was less traveled. The path was filled with snow-covered woods, less visible then the main street. We were lucky enough not to encounter other travelers along the way.

Once daylight broke we sped up or pace since the horses took to the weather well. We were in the city of Kiel within a few hours and Kristoph took the lead as we slowly rode through the streets and towards the docks. I hoped The Feuervogel was awaiting our arrival just as Kristoph had promise. We stopped and he looked around, I thought he was lost for a minute but he seemed to recognize a tavern to the left. That familiar smirk formed on his pale face as he shouted "This way!" We follow him down another alleyway and then turned right. I could see the ocean now and smelled the sea salt. It was strong but mildly refreshing. The sun was rising just over the horizon and the scene was peaceful.

Even with everything still weighing on my mind, the sea seemed to calm my nerves. Kristoph broke my peaceful thoughts when he yelled "There...over there. It's the ship" we raced to the dock. Captain Christian had kept his word and the ship was there in waiting.

She was magnificent, long, and with large yellowish sails and lanterns lighting the way up to her deck. We stopped and dismounted while the crew greeted us. They helped to unload the horses and in a bit of luck, a passerby offered us coin for them. I did not like seeing my horse sold, Geheimhalter had served me well and I would miss him dearly, but a ship was no place for him or his companions. The offer was reasonable and I was guaranteed they would be in good care.

Upon boarding, Captain Chrisman introduced himself and his stench was that of sea salt and bitterness, his mannerism also informed me that he was a hard captain without a sense of humor. He asked for the rest of our gold upfront and we paid him, then he shouted for us to settle in. "We are set to sail in a few moments so be ready." He made it clear that we were neither his guests nor part of his crew, so warm food or soft beds were not part of our deal. If we wanted any accommodations, we were to work for them. That was the catch, this Captain assumed he would assimilate us into his crew, honestly, I didn't care what this idiot had planned for us, for he would be dead once Kristoph stole the registry.

As the day broke, I heard the captain bark orders to his crew, since I never sailed before I had no idea what portside was or even the meaning of stern. However, I still watched as they hustled along the deck, raising sails, and tying ropes. I looked around and counted many men aboard, so we had the food for the trip, but to pilot such a vessel was beyond me. I tried to learn as much as I could just in case we found ourselves in need of a helmsman.

Who can foresee the outcome of such a long trip? In three days, the moon will be full and the Changing will come once again, just as it always does. Until then I will take in the sea air and dream of this new land...I will dream of America.

Thank you for reading my book. If you enjoyed My Wolf Within, please let others know by leaving a review, thank you.

More from the Journals of Wilhelm Von Krieg

Book Two 1784-1820

Book Three 1840-1882

Book Four 1902-1946

Book Five 1947-2012

To follow Ray R Wise on Instagram

https://www.instagram.com/mindmachineauthor/?hl=en

About the Author

A Columbia College graduate, Wise holds a B.A. in sound engineering with a minor in music. In 2006, he signed with DarkStar Records, by 2012 released two worldwide albums, and has been featured on multiple movie soundtracks. With the urge of expanding his creativity, Wise began writing the "My Wolf Within" series and published the first installment of the five-book saga in 2020. He resides in the suburbs of Chicago.

Made in the USA
Columbia, SC
16 April 2022